New Edition

Dark Nights

First in the Until Dawn series

JORDAN E. WALKER

New Edition

ISBN:
Paperback 978-1-954341-15-9

The views expressed in this book are solely those of the author and do not necessarily reflect the views of the publisher, and the publisher hereby disclaims any responsibility for them.

Writers' Branding
1800-608-6550
www.writersbranding.com
orders@writersbranding.com

Contents

Singer's House
Favian's Estate
Popular Tavern

Belmount
Elfroad
Resomist
Bluehaven
Westmood
Aldercrest
Silvercrest
Lonecliff
Eastrock
Greenport
Clearapal
Prryland

Cliff
River
Wood

When the darkness of night comes,
stay with me until dawn breaks...

"What is civility? In contrast, what is savagery?" the old philosopher, Edric, asked. I rolled my eyes and turned my attention elsewhere. Sitting in the small cobblestone quad with nothing but a few stone benches, there wasn't much to look at. Meanwhile, Edric stood, towering over on top of a small stool, but at the same time, small and frail. The boy sitting closest to him with a journal opened on his lap- a few notes scribbled in it neatly- raised his hand immediately. Edric nodded to him after scanning the crowd for anyone else. "What is your theory, Blaine?"

"To be civil, you must have and practice moral teachings, such as showing diplomacy instead of war. Savagery is defined as those who would fling headfirst into war without a second thought for peaceful negotiations." Blaine finished staring at the elderly man with a hopeful smile on his face. Edric nodded his head in approval before beginning to explain why Blaine's explanation was right.

"That's so asinine." Rose, my best friend sitting next to me on one of the benches, whispered in my ear. I leaned closer to her so we wouldn't get caught talking by the temperamental old man.

"Does he really think anyone cares for his lectures?" I whispered back to her, a bored frown on my face. Rose mirrored my expression with an added touch of disgust in hers.

"What does he expect we'll get from this- a touch of 'civility'?"

"He wants us to be less savage."

"Oh right, so the next time I take your apple pie, be sure to express some 'civility' and come up with a diplomatic solution, won't you?"

"Of course, you savage." we put our hands over our mouths to muffle the laughter that consumed us.

"Jayde, Rose," Edric's booming voice silenced our lighthearted banter. Rose and I both turned our attention to Edric, who has been annoying me for the past hour. "Is there something amusing about what the class is discussing that you want to share?" Rose opened her mouth to deny it, but I cut her off with a short, ridiculing laugh.

"On the contrary, I do." Edric stayed deathly quiet, his dark eyes that were hidden from my view as they sunk into his face, never breaking eye contact. "You will have to forgive me if I sound rude, but your question is absurd and, overall, ineffective. What is civility in contrast to savagery? Civility is what people in power like to flaunt and preach about while savagery is what powerful people call their enemies. More importantly, no one cares enough to even consider what you're saying to be relevant. What are you expecting a bunch of over-privileged, spoiled brats to gain from this? As I said, your lesson is completely absurd, and I see no point in why my parents are paying you to teach it. It's such a waste of money." By the time I finished, the others were whispering. I couldn't understand most of it, then again, it's not like I was going to go out of my way to find out the topic they were discussing when I have a pretty good guess of who is on their lips.

"Ms. Henryk," Edric finally spoke after a few minutes silencing the noisy lot. "Stay here after I have dismissed the class. It seems you need extra tutoring in, not only civility but respect." My smile left my lips being replaced by a deep frown. Did he really just call me disrespectful? At least I'm not the one drawing obscene pictures of him falling into a rocky lake like the guys in front of me!

"That seems like a harsh punishment for a youngster that had the courage and 'civility' to speak up." Everyone's eyes turned to a cloaked figure that suddenly appeared from the middle of the students seated on the ground. Needless to say, the old man was not happy.

"How dare you interrupt my class? Who are you?" Edric demanded, his face turning an alarming bright red. Is he about to have a heart attack? Besides, who *is* this mystery person? Their voice sounds light and feminine, so it could be a girl or a prepubescent boy.

"I'm merely an advocate for knowledge." the hooded woman- I think- clearly stated before turning their head in my direction. "I assume you are Jayde, the uncivilized, disrespectful, over-privileged, spoiled brat, correct?"

"Those are some pretty serious declarations coming from someone I don't know."

"But aren't they merely the words you and your teacher spoke?" my frown deepened. Am I really getting another lecture?

"I fail to see the point in neither your words nor the reason why you are here. Therefore, I will only tell you once more to leave, or I will be forced to call the guard to take you away." Edric threatened in a firm, no-nonsense tone. The person didn't even flinch as they let out a bellowing chuckle.

"Didn't you say that the mark of a savage lies in their inability to perform negotiations?"

"There is nothing savage about using force to get the desired outcome."

"Aren't you going back on your words now?"

"What are you attempting to say?"

"I am saying that there is no such thing as savagery and civility because human nature is not one or the other. Human nature is unpredictable, which constitutes that it is free and pure. Attempting to place a label on it will only show your inability to accept that despite your obtuse views."

"Are you saying that I am stupid?" Edric questioned, dangerously straightening his hunched back to appear taller. The woman let out a chuckle as she relaxed in her seated position, leaning back on her arms.

"If you would like to interpret my words in that way, then yes. However, in reality, that is not what I said."

"Then, by all means, explain."

"I was saying that your societal views and standards are, as you so plainly put it, stupid. No human alive is either savage or civil. We are merely what we perceive to be correct and what is correct is in the mindset of the person who believes in it. To put it in simpler terms as you require: reality is what a person believes it is. No number of lectures or any other form of teaching you come up with can change that fact." Edric stood still for a long moment, staring venomously at the woman, but, for some reason, I found myself staring at her in admiration.

This is the first time I've heard someone defend my viewpoints on how bias our society really is. I mean, come on, who honestly believes that any person would attempt to negotiate with someone who assaulted them first? No one, because any person would have given the same answer- they attacked me, so I defended myself. Anyone who says otherwise is a liar or a pacifist. Since I know for sure that Edric is everything but a pacifist, he's the former.

As of such, I don't pay attention to any of his pointless lectures. In response, Edric has labeled me his worst student- Rose being the only other rival to my position just because she associates with me. Knowing Rose as long as I have, I know she believes the same thing I do. After all, she was the first one to bring up the topic, but I also know that she would never express her thoughts out loud. Hearing someone besides me speaking the real facts to Edric is really refreshing.

"If that is what you truly believe, then allow me to explain to you the errors in your ways." Edric began with the faintest traces of a smirk. "Human nature is neither pure nor free. In fact, our nature as a species is solely governed by our selfish needs and frivolous wants. We are untamed beasts built to withstand the harsh, bitter cruelty of the world with barbaric deeds and thoughts. Our kind does not simply need direction and order, but it *craves* it. We, as humans, *crave* that of which you dare to call stupid. To put it in simpler terms for you to understand, humanity is bursting at the seams with corruption that needs to be contained. Therefore, we as a society- as a species- must enforce discipline and principle into our fellow brethren to control their impure nature."

"But isn't that what you call savagery? Aren't you refusing to negotiate with those who would not believe in the same things as you? Aren't you practicing savagery by plunging headfirst into war with those who would oppose your views? Judging you by the standards that you have set, you and your practices are savage." Edric's face contorted and twisted until a nasty scowl formed.

"I think he might be having a heart attack," Rose whispered to me.

"Who are you? Take off that hood this instance, or I will call the guard and have you arrested!" Edric half yelled in such a strained voice it really did sound like he had a heart attack.

"Sounds like it," I whispered in amusement to Rose, covering my mouth so I could hide my laughter. I mean, come on, how can anyone take Edric seriously when he looks like he's constipated?

"If that is what you wish." The hooded figure replied in unhidden amusement.

"You best." Edric gritted out.

I can most certainly guess that, whoever is underneath that hood, is smiling or laughing. The woman deliberately lifted her arms slowly, curling her fingers around the fabric covering her face. Right when she began to peel it back, a small ball fell from the confines of the hood and exploded on impact with the ground. A large cloud of smoke filled the area, stinging my eyes, and clogging my throat. I could hear Rose choking next to me, along with the rest of my classmates. When the smoke finally cleared a few seconds later, the woman was gone.

"Ugh, what was that?" Rose groaned, still coughing. Taking a deep, calming breath to test my lung function, I turned to her and patted her hard on the back once, causing her to sputter and glare at me.

"Pretty sure they're called smoke bombs, but that's just a guess considering it released smoke and all." Rose rolled her eyes at me before standing up, looking in the direction of Edric. I followed her gaze and saw him lying on the floor, mumbling before turning his hazy eyes to the sky, screaming dramatically.

"That savage! Do you see? There are savages everywhere! They must be contained! That savage will pay for this!" I could barely resist the urge to laugh as he continued his hissy fit on the ground while the teacher's pet, Blaine, knelt next to him doing everything he could to help the old man. Everyone else, after Edric stood still for a long moment, staring endlessly at the woman assessing the situation, gathered their things and left.

"Well, I guess class is over." Rose yawned, picking up her journal that fell off of her lap during the fray. She tucked the little brown book underneath her arm then turned to me. "Would you like to walk home together?" I shrugged while standing up, holding my own journal to my chest. I dusted off the back of my dress before facing Rose again.

"I guess so. I have nothing else I have to do anyway." And with that, we left Blaine and Edric in the quad.

***

After dropping Rose off at her house, I began the trek to my own. It wasn't far away- half a mile or so from Rose's. However, the scene with the woman and Edric plagued my mind.

Savages and civility genuinely don't exist now that I think about it. Even those who claim to be high and mighty with civility and decorum can be the worst of savages. I know it's true because I see the evidence of it every day with my own family wealthy nobles with high standing in the government. My father, the almighty Ethan Henryk, is a part of the king's council of loyal advisors. Every man in the country- and probably in the continent- admires him and more than likely would kill to be him.

My mother, Evelyn Henryk, is the perfect housewife and not to mention very beautiful. She cares for her two children, my little brother and me, with the utmost affection and unconditional love. Every woman alive model themselves after her and every wife copies her actions to create the perfect home environment. My little brother, Aric Henryk, is the ideal son. He is top of his class and can master any subject you throw at him. Then there's me, Jayde Henryk, who is the perfect daughter and the ideal heiress to the vast fortune and fame of the Henryk family. Every boy in the continent is fighting at our doorstep just to get the chance to speak and attempt to court me. At least, that's what it looks like on the surface.

In reality, my family is plagued with savagery. My father is a traditional maniac. Our entire family must be perfect, or else he will leave without a second thought as to what will happen to us. My mother is a heartless puppet who merely obeys and does whatever my father tells her to. I'm not even sure how much she truly cares for Aric and me. I mean, she says she loves us occasionally before we go to bed and seldom when we leave for classes in the morning, but shouldn't she say it more often? Aric… well, he's exactly how he should be. He's a seven-year-old boy whose only goal in life is to make his parents proud and to take care of his elder sister. He once even told me that he wants to be a part of the guard so he can complete both of his goals.

I, on the other hand, am the black sheep of the family only because I'm smart enough to see the flaws and brave- or maybe even foolish- enough to call my parents out on them. The amount of times I've been punished by my parents for calling them a degrading name is too many for me to count. As of such, we've grown an unusual relationship- they boast about my academic accomplishments in public while in private, they scorn me for everything I do or say. In retaliation, I admonish them for their failures at being caring, loving parents. That's just how it works in my family.

"Hello, Jayde." my gaze turned across the street to our neighbor's son, Hadyn. Inwardly I sighed.

"Hello, Hadyn," I called back with as much fake pleasantry as I could muster. I mean, come on this happens every day! I walk home, I try to go inside, Hadyn calls me, tries to ask me on a date, I decline with as much 'civility' as I can, then slam the door in his face before he can make a bigger fool of himself.

Does he have any creativity?

"My mother is planning to have a picnic in a few days, would you be interested in coming with me?" My smile never wavered as I began to walk back towards my door. It wasn't until I felt the handle in my grasp that I spoke knowing precisely what was about to leave my lips.

"I would love to if I had the time. I'm afraid my family and I will be in the capital that day for an important meeting with the king my father has to attend to, maybe another time?" Right before he could speak, I closed the door letting out an annoyed sigh. When will he ever learn?

"-the queen assured Jax that she will hold on to the jewel. Years went by, and Jax became old and frail. It was on the day his sons became adults that he told them the story of the queen. He told them to never forget about it and to keep the memory of it alive through their children until the day came that they may have to go back to the queen and get it." I heard Aric recite as he sat at the kitchen table, swinging his legs back and forth, staring at a spot on the wall with mild interest. I turned my gaze from him to look at the clothed back of my mother as she washed dishes and seemingly ignored every word. Rage built up in my heart as Aric turned his hopeful eyes to our mother's back and asked, voice filled with hope, "How did I do, mommy?" She stopped in her robotic motions gazing over her shoulder at him.

"You forgot parts of the story. You must remember every detail, or else your father will not be pleased." The sight of Aric's bright brown eyes turning downwards in dejection made my blood boil with hate.

"I think you did an awesome job," I spoke loudly, drawing both of their attention. Aric's eyes lit up in happiness as my mother's expression stayed aloof and indifferent like always.

"Jay!" He shouted, jumping from his chair and running to me, but our mother clapped her hands- loud and sharp- stopping him in his tracks.

"What have I told you about doing that?" She barked out, staring icily at Aric's back. He took a brave, deep breath and slowly turned, keeping his eyes downcast.

"That a respectable boy greets others calmly and with dignity." He repeated, not once lifting his eyes to her grey ones. Our mother nodded before lifting her eyes to my glare. She didn't even flinch.

"I've told you before not to nourish this type of behavior."

"And I've told you before that Ricky is a seven-year-old child. He should and will act like one." I turned my gaze down to Aric's downcast head and wrapped my arms around him, pulling him to my chest. Softly I blew on the back of his neck, causing him to erupt in laughter.

"Stop it, Jay!" He laughed, trying to shake out of my embrace. A loud smack on the table brought our attention to our mother, glaring heatedly at me wielding a wooden spoon in her hand.

"I will not tolerate your blatant disrespect for my authority." I stood up straight, not releasing Aric from my embrace while I stared her down defiantly.

"Funny you should mention that. Today in our lesson we spoke about the difference between civility and savagery. Going off what I learned today, you and father are just two people plagued with the curse of human nature that we all have. It just so happens you two are more savage than the rest of us." An angry fire shot through her eyes as she took a threatening step forward.

"I will not-"

"Do you know what else I learned today, Ricky?" I asked Aric, completely ignoring our mother, who was now fuming with anger. Aric looked very uncomfortable but shook his head anyway. "I learned what an old man looks like when he has to poop!"

"Jayde!" I laughed along with Aric, who was trying his best not to as our mother glared dangerously at us. "Jayde, I will not tolerate you corrupting your brother any longer. Go up to your room and wait for me." I gave her a leveling look as a smirk came to my lips.

"Isn't the first sign of savagery not being able to negotiate?" Her eyes narrowed into slits. I grunted in amusement, fully turning my attention to Aric. "Why don't we go to my room to go over that outdated fairytale, okay?" Aric's eyes lit up at the thought, and he nodded his head vigorously. I smiled, taking his hand before heading upstairs without saying another word to our so-called mother.

***

When we made it to my room, Aric happily ran in and jumped onto my bed with a burst of childish laughter lingering in his wake. A wide smile was permanently on his face as he glanced around my simply furnished room with open, curious eyes. My anger subsided as I quietly closed the door with a soft click.

"How was your day today, Ricky?" I asked, strolling over to him and lying down on the bed next to him while he sat cross-legged. His eyes lit up from the simple question as he animatedly told me the trials and tribulations of his day.

"It started off when I went to school. Ms. Laura was very nice to us- she brought us cookies and even read a story about this little old lady who lived in a shoe! After that, she gave us a philosophy question to answer. The question was about how a person was similar to an animal. She said I came up with the best explanation."

"What did you say?" I asked, bemused by his intense happiness by something so simple.

"I said a person is like a worm because we all start off as babies. We are all little and full of hopes and dreams about what we want to do when we're bigger. Then, we turn into cocoons and, by that time, we have to decide what we will be. By the end, we turn into beautiful butterflies, and we are the person who we always wanted to be." He finished with a spark in his eyes that warmed my heart.

"How did a little seven-year-old like you come up with something like that?" His face twisted in his deep thoughts before he nodded his head coming to an acceptable answer.

"I got it from you! I remember you telling me something like that a few months ago when daddy got mad at me for going to their room during the thunderstorm." He finished, his voice growing softer and less happy. A frown marred my features as I sat up and stared deep into his eyes.

"What have I told you at least a thousand times before?"

"Not to listen to what mother and father say."

"So why are you now?" he stared off towards the door.

"I don't want to make anyone angry, but I don't know how to make everyone happy." A sigh broke through my lips as I grabbed both sides of his face and forced him to look at me.

"Ricky, no matter what you do, you will always make me happy. As long as you're the person you want to be and not what others think you should. You are still a little worm, but you're turning into a cocoon with so much greatness I'm worried about what will happen to the rest of the world when you hatch into a butterfly." Aric's eyes slowly turned to mine. "Besides, our parents may seem like cold-hearted people, but deep down in their hearts, they care and love us." He blinked slowly before letting out a soft sigh.

"Are you sure?" I grunted, letting out a cocky huff that brought a smile to his face.

"Of course- have you forgotten who I am?" He let out a childish laugh as I began to tickle him beneath his ribcage.

"No! I haven't forgotten!" He laughed, trying to escape. I laughed along with him, pulling him into a warm hug.

"I love you, Ricky." He chuckled as he wrapped his smaller arms around me.

"I love you too, Jay." I gave him a tight squeeze before releasing him. I flicked his nose playfully, and he whined in retaliation, rubbing his sore nose. I laughed just as my door creaked open. Our mother stepped into the room, leaving the door open. She watched us with indifferent eyes. Still, I could easily see some form of bright light within those grey depths identical to my own.

"Aric," She called. He cautiously glanced at me, and when I nodded, he puffed out his little chest and turned brave eyes to face our mother.

"Yes, mother?"

"Go to your room while I speak to your sister, please." Aric nodded, giving me a quick, tight hug before running out. Our mother watched him leave before turning her attention to me. She closed the door and walked further in, settling herself in the lone lounge chair in the corner next to the window overlooking the vast space of open grass that made up the backyard.

Neither of us spoke. We just sat in complete and utter silence. I stared at my mother, waiting for her to say something while she stared almost longingly out of the window at the wide-open space just beyond it. It was almost like she was wishing that she could be out there- running in the field entirely and utterly free.

Just like a worm dreaming of becoming a butterfly.

"I love you." She suddenly said, bringing me out of my musings. I blinked confusedly at her.

"What?"

"I love you." She repeated, turning her gaze to me. Her eyes were much softer. Her face held so many emotions that generally are void. She actually looks motherly. "You know that, right?"

"That's what I tell myself and Aric." She nods before standing up and slowly coming towards me. She stopped just a foot away, forcing me to strain my neck to look at her. Reaching out a hand, she softly placed it on my right cheek and began to smooth her thumb over the skin.

"Even though you may defy your father and me- even though we may argue, I love you. I want you to know that whatever it is that you wish to do- no matter what it is- I will love and support you." My mouth opened slightly in complete shock. Did she just say that I could be whatever I wanted? And did she really say that with sincerity?

"I... love you too." A small, sad smile formed on her lips as she let her hand fall back to her side.

"Dinner is almost ready. Ethan will be home soon. You are free to do as you wish until then, alright?" I nodded, blinking distractedly.

"Yeah, alright." I absently replied, shaking my head slightly. Still, by the time my mind stopped reeling from the out of character conversation, she was gone.

***

Just like she said, dinner was ready in a little over ten minutes. My father walked through the door when my mother was putting the food on the table, but he wasn't alone. Trailing behind him was his closest business partner, Layne Pierce.

"Uncle Layne!" Did I forget to mention he's our godfather? The elder man smiled down at Aric as the young boy ran to him. Before my mother could scold him, Layne scooped him into his arms.

"Hey champ, how have you been?"

"Good! I got praised today in class for my philosophy explanation." Layne's smile grew as he ruffled the little boy's hair.

"Still the little genius I see? What need do you have for school when you're so smart?" Aric laughed in absolute bliss before Layne placed him back on his feet. He patted Aric on the back once before turning his attention to me. "Good afternoon, little heartbreaker."

"Good afternoon, you dirty politician." We both shared a hearty laugh.

"Still as sharp-tongued as ever I see."

"And you're still as manic as always."

"Mr. Pierce," my mother cut in, giving me a sharp look. "What is the meaning of your visit today?" Layne turned his attention to my mother, a more polite smile on his face.

"Ethan here owes me a few documents. After that, I'll be on my way." My mother didn't speak again. She glanced at my father, who did nothing but turn and disappeared into his study next to the staircase.

"What are you planning to do with the documents?"

"Jayde!" my mother snapped at me.

"What?" I snapped back. Seriously, what did I do?

"I'm planning to take a trip to Rosesea next week. There's just a little business I need to take care of before."

"Awesome, can I come with you?"

"Jayde!" a soft laugh left his lips.

"Not this time, heart breaker." He said fondly. By this time, my father came back from his study wielding a thick file of papers.

"This is everything that you need to know." The tightness in my father's voice was not lost on me as he passed over the file. Layne smiled, nodding gratefully.

"Thank you. I'll see you later." Layne smacked his shoulder as a goodbye before turning to the rest of us. "Goodbye, Henryks! You shall stay on my mind until the next time I see you!"

"Goodbye, Uncle Layne!" Aric happily yelled.

"See you later." He waved at the both of us before sweeping out the door. Once the door closed, my father turned and walked towards the table. Before sitting down, he went over to my mother and gave her a peck on the lips. He even pulled out her chair and pushed it back in when she sat down! Usually, he wouldn't even bother looking at us before sitting down and eating, but today? Is the apocalypse happening?

"Hello, Evelyn, Jayde, Aric." He greeted as he sat down at the head of the table. It took everything I had not to allow my jaw to hit the ground. Seriously, what is going on? What conspiracy am I missing out on?

"Welcome home, daddy!" Aric shouted, not wanting to miss out on the uncharacteristic semi-warm greeting our father directed towards us. Our father turned his eyes to him and grunted in a strange form of a response.

"What did you do today, son?" He asked as he began to eat. Aric's eyes lit up as he repeated his story from earlier.

Throughout his long soliloquy, both of our parents paid close attention to every detail. They even went as far as to ask questions about certain things and stayed engrossed in every word that left his lips. Though I was itching to question them on their odd behavior, the look of utmost joy and unadulterated happiness on Aric's face kept me silent. What kind of sister would I be if I took this small amount of pleasure from him? So, for the rest of dinner, I held my tongue and ate in silence. Even when our father turned his attention to me after Aric was finished, I refrained from telling him about the hooded woman. That would surely send him hurling back into his old ways, and that happiness Aric is basking in would melt away.

"It was like every other day, extraordinarily normal."

II

The monstrous sound of thunder woke me with a startling fright. Looking out my window, the rain hammered against the glass, and the dark grey clouds looming threatening above showed no signs of going anywhere soon. A sigh left my lips as I rubbed my eyes, the sleep stuck in them, causing an irritating itch. Letting out a tired yawn, I glanced to my side, expecting to see Aric cowering next to me, but when I saw empty space, a frown settled on my lips.

Kicking back the warm comforter, I climbed out of bed and stepped out of my room, fully intending to go in search of Aric. Walking to the door next to mine, I knocked once calling out for him softly. When he didn't respond, my frown deepened before pushing the door open only to see him lying in bed, the covers pulled over his head. I sighed in resignation before stepping into the room, leaving the door open.

"Ricky, what are you doing?" I called, stopping next to his bed. I leaned over his still body when he didn't answer me. Another sigh left my lips. I put my hands on my hips and half-smiled. "Honestly, what have I told you at least a thousand times before? If you're scared, you can come to my room and sleep there." Still no response. My frown came back in full force.

"Ricky?" No response.

"Ricky?" Annoyed, I gripped the blanket covering his face and snatched it off, revealing his sleeping face.

A horrible knot twisted in my gut when I looked at his neck. A bone stuck out like a sore thumb that wasn't supposed to be that way. The skin of his neck was twisted in an unnatural pattern. There was a little blood coming from a puncture wound that the bone created showing its white color.

"Ricky..." I whispered, afraid of what was going through my head was the harsh reality I was now facing. He couldn't possibly... be dead, right? He could just be sleeping- his eyes are still closed!

I shook his shoulder gently. When he didn't respond, my breathing increased, and I desperately shook him. He still didn't respond. Trying hard not to panic. I took a step away from him and closed my eyes tightly. I pinched the skin of my arm, roughly causing a welt. After the pain registered in my brain, I opened my eyes, expecting to wake up in my bed from this terrible nightmare. However, the sight of Aric still lying motionlessly in his bed felt like a bucket of ice hitting me in the face. Tears streamed down my face, my breath coming in short, painful huffs.

"Ricky!" I screamed, falling to my knees next to his bed. Wrapping my arms around his small, frail body, I cradled him to my chest, rocking him.

The tears continued to pour down my face as thoughts- memories shoved their way to the forefront of my mind. They kept bombarding my consciousness until I was no longer in Aric's room, but I was in my own It was dark outside, and Aric couldn't sleep after having a nightmare. So, I set up a white sheet on the wall and lit a candle, placing a broken cup around it to focus the light on the sheet. Aric sat on the floor, staring at it expectantly.

"What are you doing, Jay?" He had asked, turning his head to glance over his shoulder at me with curious eyes.

"Stop being so impatient and watch." I laughed in response. Folding my hands in front of the light, creating a shadow of a dog against the sheet. Aric gasped in awe wholly enraptured.

"It's a puppy!" He exclaimed, swirling his head around with a smile bright enough to light up the night sky.

"What did you think it was?" I laughed, twisting my hands until a bird was formed on the wall. His face continued to light up in complete awe as he twirled around completely towards me, a spark in his eyes.

"Can you show me how to do that too?" He asked, his voice filled with hope. I rolled my eyes and nodded.

"Even if I say no, you would bother me until I did anyway." A grin covered his face stretching from ear to ear. He crawled his way over, settling himself across from me. He was bouncing up and down on his knees as he bit his bottom lip, trying hard to contain his glee. I chuckled at him before holding up my hands in a specific way after instructing him to copy my motions.

For the rest of the night, we created different stories using shadow puppets. The only other times I've ever seen Aric that happy was when our parents finally showed him the small amount of attention at last night's dinner. The other was the moment he finally said his first word. That day, I can remember as vividly as the day I taught him shadow puppets.

He was merely a toddler- barely one and a half years old- when he was beginning to learn how to speak. Our parents didn't bother for long with him opting to hire people to do it for them, so they didn't have to waste time. Even at the tender age of ten, I knew the treatment our parents showed us was wrong. So I took it upon myself to be that mother figure to my baby brother that our own mother neglected to fill.

"Come on, Ricky- it isn't that hard." I encouraged calling him by the nickname I gave him.

Back then, I was more openly defiant and immediately declared that my brother's name was Ricky. I got into an argument with my parents over it, but in the end, I ignored every word they said and continued to call Aric by the name I gave him.

"Just say it, Ricky. Say 'food.'" I prompted again, getting slightly irritated by the baby gibberish the insufferable bundle of flesh continued to recite. For the past week, he's been making the same incoherent sound instead of the simple word. Honestly, why is it so hard to teach toddler's anything-

"Jay…" My ranting stopped as I stared bewildered at the toddler before me as he giggled in immense joy at nothing.

"What did you say?"

"Jay!" He shouted louder, throwing his chubby baby arms in the air towards me, wanting to be picked up. Slowly, a smile etched across my lips as I eagerly scooped him up and cradled him in my arms, blowing air onto his belly tickling him. A gurgle left his lips in what can only be described as a baby's version of laughing. "Jay!"

"That's right, I'm Jay," I whispered into his chubby cheek as I began to rock him back and forth. "And I promise I will always take care of you, my little Ricky." If only I knew then what would happen to him, I would have saved him, but then again, how can I have saved him when I had no idea what would happen? How could I ever imagine that something this horrific would happen to my dear baby brother?

A haunting screech echoed throughout the house but was slightly muffled from the pounding rain. Squeezing my eyes closed, I took in a deep breath before laying Aric's head back down against his pillow. One last fat tear fell from my eyes as I pulled the cover over his head with a shaking hand. Bending down, I kissed his covered forehead squeezing my eyes closed to keep my tears at bay, but in the end, I lost that battle.

"I love you… Ricky." I sobbed before taking a shaky breath. Standing up straight, I stared unseeingly at the covered body of my baby brother.

As I heard glass shattering downstairs, a wave of rage and hate consumed me. Is the person who murdered my brother still inside this house? I hope he is because when I find him, I'm going to bury him six feet under! Moving towards Aric's wardrobe, I reached inside and pulled out the wooden bat tucked into the corner. The memory of when I gave it to him tried to slither to the forefront of my mind, but I forced it back using my rage. Tightening my grip on the bat, I quickly made my way out of Aric's room, sparing one final glance at the door before shutting it silently.

An unnatural calm came over me as I slowly made my way to the stairs. Was it because of the agony, denial, guilt, anger, and remorse filling me all at once? Whatever it was, I was thankful for it. It made what I was planning to do so much easier. Taking a smooth breath, I peered down the stairs only for my mouth to fly open and tears to spill into my eyes once again. The loud clatter of the bat hitting the ground barely registered in my mind as the sight stunned me to my very core.

My mother lay on the floor with lifeless eyes staring blankly at some distant object. Blood began to pool around her from a wound I couldn't see. Leaning over her body, was my father. He was on his knees, and his head hung limply, blocking his face from my view. There was a lot of blood on him, and I couldn't tell if it was his or my mother's. Slowly, my eyes traveled away from their bodies to the third one- a stranger- laying only a few feet away from my mother. He was covered from head to toe in black with his face covered in a mask. Littered around him was pieces of a broken vase that I can only guess one of my parents used to subdue him with before they were killed themselves.

Killed.

My entire family… is gone.

"No…" The broken sob escaped my lips before I could stop it. Almost immediately, my father's head snapped in my direction, bringing a scream from my throat. He blinked like he couldn't see me. My hands trembled against my chest as I took an uneasy step forward. "Father?" He didn't respond. He turned his head back down to my mother's body and leaned down towards her face.

He whispered something into her ear, which I knew she wouldn't be able to hear before placing a lingering kiss onto her forehead. He stood tall, his breathing and disposition completely calm. Slowly, he turned his head to me and motioned for me to come downstairs to him. As if on autopilot, I moved towards him, stopping a few feet away, never taking my eyes off of my mother's body.

"What… why…" the words just wouldn't form. What happened? *Why* did this happen? *Who* is that man? *Why* did he do this? Did someone send him? Why did he have to kill my brother and mother? Was he planning on killing all of us?

Why? Why? Why?!

"Jayde," my eyes lifted to meet my father's only to, for the third time tonight, freeze. What is that glint in his eyes? Sadness? Grief? Anger? No, I know what that look is. It's *regret*!

"What did you do?" I whispered in disbelief as tears began to build up in my eyes once again.

"We don't have time for this-"

"What did you do, you bastard?" I screamed, shoving him roughly and pounding on his chest with all the strength, frustration, and hatred I held within myself.

"Jayde, stop this instant!" He snapped at me, grabbing my wrists painfully and shoving them away. My mind, clouded in my frenzy, wouldn't-couldn't- register his words, and I lashed out at him using my legs. I kicked at him, trying with every fiber of my being to force him to feel *something*. Why is he acting so calm about this? He shouldn't be this calm!

"What did you do?" I screamed at him again and again. Fed up, he tightened his hold on my wrists and spun me around. Winding his arms around my torso, so he held down my arms, he lifted me from my feet. I swung my legs wildly, trying with all my might to kick him anywhere, but I never made contact.

He carried me outside in the pouring rain getting us both drenched in its wrath. The shock of freezing droplets cleared my mind causing all the events that just happened to come to a standstill in my consciousness. Both my brother and mother were murdered. The murderer responsible is now dead as well, but why? What have they done to deserve this? I know for a fact that they did nothing to deserve their fate. It *has* to be something that my father did- it *has* to!

"What did you do...?" I whispered, absently letting my head hang. Tears began to flood my cheeks once again, only to be washed away by the rain.

"I almost thought you didn't make it, Mr. Henryk." A familiar gruff voice half-heartedly joked. I lifted my head up as my father sat me down on my feet in front of a common carriage. A large buff man stood beside it dressed in a trench coat that grazed the ground and a hat that worked as a shield for his face from the rain. He held the door to the carriage open, a sad grin tugging on his lips, his hazel eyes jaded, not allowing a single form of emotion to leak through.

"Have you completed the instructions I gave to you, Kale?"

"Of course, sir." He grunted as my father climbed into the carriage. "Everything is in order. By morning, everyone in town will think the entire Henryk family was murdered during a home invasion."

"Everyone will think..." I cut in, my voice sounding as if I were a haunting spirit and not a living breathing girl. Kale turned his gaze to me, his eyes never once showing any form of pity or empathy.

"If I were to tell people the truth, they would all-"

"That's enough, Kale." My father snapped, sending a nasty glare Kale's way before turning it on me. "Jayde, get into the carriage. Now." My eyes slowly turned up to meet his gaze.

"No."

"Jayde-"

"Tell me- what did you do, and why do you have this elaborate escape plan? Why did my brother and mother have to die? What did you do to cause this?" His face stilled. He shifted his attention away from me and on an invisible spot on the opposite wall.

"We are going to Rosesea. There are plenty of small villages there that have no knowledge of events that transpire in Clearapal. We can disappear there."

"But *why*?" I croaked. Without even sparing me a glance, my father sat up straight, keeping his eyes averted.

"Kale, please assist Jayde into the carriage so we may leave as scheduled." My eyes widened. Did he… just blow me off like that? Did he do that even *after* everything that has happened?

"Sorry, little lady," Kale stated before gripping me underneath my armpits. He lifted me up until I was seated next to my father in the carriage. Kale climbed in across from us, closing the door behind him. Once he was settled, he knocked on the wall, separating us from the driver. A muffled snap of reins was heard before the carriage lurched forward.

Throughout the whole experience, my brain refused to process any more than it already has. Just the thought of attempting to try and make sense of the conversation going on between bodyguard and employer made my brain shut down in fear of causing some kind of permanent damage. Vaguely, I can hear them speaking about the man who sent the assassin. Though they didn't mention any names, it's clear to me that my father knows exactly who sent that man to our home. Even Kale showed signs of knowing who they are.

So why won't they go after him? Why are we running away?

The thoughts slipped silently into my conscious and vanished before they could take root and cause a mental break down. I just stared blankly out of the crack of the window that wasn't covered by the blinds. The rain let up slightly, and, before long, it stopped.

"I wouldn't suggest staying in the same place for too long. He will most certainly send out more men to get rid of you when he figures out you're still alive. I'm not sure if the little lady will be in too much danger, but I will do as much as I can on my end to give you enough time to disappear."

"Good. Make sure that Evelyn and Aric are buried properly."

"I will, Mr. Henryk."

"Thank you. Your final payment is in the locked drawer of my office. I trust you know where the key to open it is."

"Yes." My brain stopped processing their words after that. The rain completely stopped falling, being replaced by a dreary mist that covered the darkened early morning. The distant sound of waves crashing against a shore forced me back to reality. We were nearing a dock- a dock that will take us far away.

"I've always hated boats," I whispered to no one leaning my head against the door, my mind returning to its blank slate.

III

"I can guarantee you at least a few days. After that, I don't know what will happen." Kale said as he helped me out of the carriage. I think I mumbled a thank you, but I can't be sure. My mind is so numb; I can only listen to what was happening around me without processing anything.

"That should be enough time." Vaguely I felt a hand go on my shoulder, maneuvering me further away from the carriage as Kale climbed back inside. "Thank you for your service, Kale." He grunted, turning his sharp eyes to me.

"Take care, little lady."

"You as well." He blinked at me for a second before letting out a low snort.

"It'll get easier- you just have to learn to cope with the pain. You're a smart girl, little lady, I'm sure you'll learn to manage." Not all of his words stuck in my brain, but the main idea was prevalent enough. He anticipated my silence as he closed the door to the carriage, and, a few seconds later, it pulled off.

"Come." My father barked before walking away. I just followed silently behind him, holding my head down low, trying not to think, but somehow the thoughts keep shoving their way into my mind.

Why? Why did this happen? Why is my father and Kale *lying* about what happened? Why won't they *tell* me what happened? *Why*? That's all I want to know- *why*? At least if I know that, then I'll know why my brother and mother were taken from me. My feet stopped moving, my back ramrod straight.

Is that why they were acting so strange last night? Did they know this would happen? Were they trying to leave Aric and me with the memory that they were good parents before the deed was done? Did they know there was going to be an assassin? My eyes widened.

My mother and father both knew this would happen! They knew someone was coming to kill us! They *knew*!

"What did you do?" My voice came out strong and confident- the opposite of how I feel. My father, again, ignored my question opting to push me closer to the ship anchored at the end of the dock. Twirling around, I smacked his hand away from me and gave him a look that showed what I really thought of him. "Answer me!"

"Jayde, you are-"

"Did you make someone angry?" I shot out, cutting him off. When his jaw tightened, my heart sunk. "You did, didn't you?"

"Jayde-"

"Do you even care that you caused your own son and wife's death?"

"Shut your mouth this instant, or I will leave you here." He snapped, glaring at me like a wronged spirit come to life. My eyes widened before they lowered. Knowing him, he wouldn't even look back as he left. "Get on the ship and don't speak of this again." Lifting my eyes, grey clashed with cold brown orbs, mine stinging with tears.

"I hate you." With that said, I turned on my heels. I boarded the ship, my brain refusing to acknowledge anything happening around me.

***

I don't remember when or how, but when I awoke from the trance, I was standing in the ship's captain's cabin. My father stood beside me, checking the pocket watch he always kept on him. Out of reflex, I averted my eyes, making a noise of disgust in the back of my throat. He heard, but he ignored it.

Just like he's ignoring everything else.

"Ethan, ye ole bat!" A tall, lean man greeted loudly, entering from a hidden door behind the tarp on the other side of his desk. He made his way to my father, giving him a chaste embrace before turning to me.

"My word," he breathes dramatically removing his hat that strongly resembled a pirate's and placed it over his heart. "I do see we have a beautiful young lass on the ship." He moved his gaze back to my father. "Is she ye'r daughter, mate?"

"Yes."

"Ye don't say," the unknown man turned back to me and performed a swooping bow. "I be Captain Jin. At ye'r service anytime, young madam." he took my hand and kissed the back of it.

"It's a pleasure to meet you, Captain Jin. My name is Jayde, Jayde Henryk." His eyes lit up in recognition, his head flying back with a hearty laugh escaping his lips.

"So, you be the lass I hear the boys in the tavern harp and moan about? Well, now that I look at ya, ye are as beautiful as they exaggerated, but are ye as devilish as they say, I wonder?" He rubbed his chin, a playful twinkle in his green eyes. A short amused grunt left my throat as I scanned his figure with curious eyes.

Now that I look at him, he does resemble a pirate. He had two pistols strapped on both sides of his hips and two extras on his chest. A cutlass lay just above the gun on his left hip. Draped over his shoulders, he wore a long trench coat that held numerous pockets. A leather belt wrapped lowly on his waist, about four small pouches tied to it. Other than the silver-plated armor, baggy black breaches, and grey undershirt, he wore high rising black leather boots.

"Are you a pirate, Captain Jin?" Another bellowing laugh came from him as he replaced his hat on top of his tied back light brown hair, a smile never leaving his face.

"What gives ya that idea, lass?"

"I don't know. It surely wouldn't be the clothes, numerous weapons, word choice, or the way you smell like saltwater." A crooked grin formed on his face, his hands resting on his hips.

"What a lass!" He barked out, smacking my father on the back with more force then he intended. "You raised her right, mate!" my father didn't say a thing. He just stood there like the monster he truly is.

"You didn't answer my question." I butted in giving all of my attention to Captain Jin. If he noticed the intense atmosphere between my father and me, he didn't say anything. The grin never left his face once he angled his body towards me while still being able to see my father out of the corner of his eye.

"Aye, that's right, lass." He contemplated mildly taking a step towards his desk and away from my father. "Aye, it is true that I once be a pirate. I sailed all across this world and even seen creatures that'd give ye nightmares. I've even met a few beauties- whether they be human or nay. Alas, I had to give up that life. Now, I be a simple mercenary who, from time to time, provide safe transport to or fro the civilized world of Clearapal or the nobly savage Rosesea. It be a simple life, but it be a content one."

"From the sounds of it, the one you had before sounds like heaven." *Just like the one I had…*

"Aye, but that be the mere surface, lass. There be things I once had to do to survive that I will only share during my judgment day."

"What was the deciding factor that made you leave the life of a pirate?"

"A wish." His eyes darkened slightly.

"A wish?"

"Aye, a wish be the reason."

"Why would you let something as silly and ridiculous as that change your life?" I half-laughed but nearly choked on my saliva when his face stayed as dangerous as it was when he started.

"A wish is powerful, lass." His eyes took on a hazy tint as he seemed to look through me at some distant memory. "Be careful as to whom ye speak of ye'r wishes to. Ye don't know who ye could be speakin' to- they may end up twisting it into something dark."

"Sounds like a fairytale to me." A low chuckle rumbled through his chest. He straightened, the twinkle back in his eyes.

"Aye, I guess so, lass." Petting his cutlass on his hip and lowering his head with his eyes closed. Suddenly, his head snapped up, showing off a dazzling smile. "That be enough reminiscin', time to take ye to ye'r quarters so we can set sail!" he walked past us, slamming the door to the cabin open. "Land lovers on deck!" he shouted to his crew, who yelled in response.

Before my father could even begin to start moving, I rushed out to the deck, waiting patiently for Captain Jin to lead the way to the cabin. Hopefully, he will abandon my father in the room alone. In the end, he held the door open until my father walked through. I turned my eyes away in disgust. Why can't he just stay here and leave me alone like he wants to?

"This way, lass." Captain Jin smoothly glided passed me, and towards the middle of the ship where a door half embedded into the deck lay. He opened it, revealing a set of stairs that twisted towards a hall filled with seven cabin doors- three on each side and one straight ahead.

"Captain-"

"Which one is ours?" I quickly asked, not wanting to hear my father's corrupted voice.

"Straight ahead, lass."

"Thank you, ex-pirate Captain Jin." His grin grew as he nodded. He started to make his way upstairs when he paused and dipped his head down. "It's not as much room as ye be used to. Use the other rooms if ye must." He turned once again to go back upstairs before quickly ducking his head back down. "Oh, and one more thing, lass! Is this ye'r first time out on the big blue?" My father opened his mouth to speak, but I cut him off with a loud snort.

"Considering my father has some kind of vendetta against change that can bring happiness and joy to his 'beloved' family, yes, this is my first time at sea." His bellowing laughter echoed loudly through the hall caused me to wince slightly at the sheer volume. How loud can this ex-pirate captain be!

"That lass of ye'rs is something not of this world mate! I like her!" He laughed, wiping at his eye. Taking a deep breath, Captain Jin looked at me with a crooked grin. "But in all seriousness, take care not to inhale the alluring scent of the ocean. It can bring on accursed visions to those it calls strangers." And with that, he finally disappeared up the steps, the loud bang of the door closing confirming he eventually left. My father cleared his throat, abolishing the smile that was on my face.

"Jayde," He started straightening his clothing until he deemed himself decent. He didn't bother looking at me as he focused solely on whatever was in the pocket of his trench coat. "When we get to Rosesea, we will-"

"That's very convenient that you already have an escape plan. It would've been helpful not even three hours ago when my baby brother and mother were killed during a 'tragic home invasion.' Though, if I remember correctly, Kale said that both of us died as well. So, unless I am a phantom or all of this is some sick twisted dream, why in the world would you have some kind of elaborate escape plan like this?" His jaw tightened.

"Jayde, what have I told you about-"

"I remember what you said. Maybe I just want you to leave like I know you want to." I spat before turning my back on him, marching straight to the end of the hallway.

"Jayde!" I ignored his call, shoving open the door and slamming it closed behind me. I hate him. I hate every fiber that makes up *him*! Why won't he just tell me?

Why!

***

I don't know when or how, but the next thing I remember is waking up in a sunny field covered in sunflowers and wheat. Confused, I sat up and looked around me uneasily. Aren't I supposed to be on a ship? Am I dreaming?

"Jay!" My heart skipped a beat. It *can't* be! I snapped my head in the direction of the little voice I know far too well. Sure enough, Aric- my little Ricky was running full speed towards me with a bright smile on his face, and a joy-filled twinkle in his eyes.

"Ricky…" I breathe, unable to do anything besides stare at him. This… is this real? Oh, please let it be real!

"Jay!" He hollered, jumping up in the air with his arms outspread towards me. On reflex, I shot my arms out and caught him underneath his armpits just in time. He giggled in absolute bliss as he buried his face into my shoulder. He feels so real- so *alive*.

"Ricky, what are we-"

"Mother and Father said we can play hide-and-seek as long as we stay where they can see us!" He pulled back with the smile still frozen on his face. I couldn't do anything but stare. A part of me knew that this couldn't- that this *can't* be real, but a more significant, stronger piece forced me to believe.

"Where is... mother and father?" My voice nearly cracked. She's supposed to be dead. Is she somehow alive too?

"They're over there!" Aric shouted, pointing his chubby finger in the distance. My eyes adjusted to the onslaught of the bright sun rays until I could make out the sight of my mother and father lounging together on a blanket.

My father sat with one leg extended out in front of him, and the other bent to prop up a novel on his knee that is, most likely, about politics and government business. My mother lay by his side on her back, and her head propped up on his outstretched leg as she knitted what looked to be a scarf. Occasionally, she lifted her chin to look at her husband and ask a question with a smile on her face. My father would pause to turn his head downwards and respond to her, adoration shining in his eyes. It looked as if they're actually *happy*. We all look like we are genuinely blissful.

"Please don't let this be a dream..." I whispered almost inaudibly.

"What's a dream, Jay?"

"Nothing." I turned my eyes back to my baby brother. The sincerest smile I've ever shown warming my heart. "It's absolutely nothing." I kissed his temple to which he laughed and wiggled his way out of my arms.

"Go hide, Jay! I wanna count first!" He excitedly shouted with a determined haze over his eyes.

"Alright, but don't get scared when you can't find me!" I laughed.

"I'm not going to get scared! Besides, I could find you blindfolded!" He argued back, puffing up his chest. I laughed, flicking him on the nose, eliciting a surprised squeak from him.

"Then try and find me!" I challenged before taking off in a random direction. "Don't peek!" I shouted over my shoulder. I faintly heard him call that he wouldn't before he started his counting.

A rush of ecstasy filled me as I ran through the tall flowers. The wind blowing in my face throwing my hair into a wild dance, my heart pumping in my ears, and best of all, the sound of Aric's *voice* brought on a feeling I will never forget. It was such a feeling that words such as bliss or elated couldn't contain. This feeling is in a league of its own. For the first time in who knows how long, I actually feel like I have a *family*. A *family*.

"Ten… nine… eight…" Hearing Aric nearing the end to his counting, I slammed my body into the ground, effectively concealing myself within the tall vegetation. I had to put a hand over my mouth to contain my giggles as I silently waited for Aric to finish counting.

"Five…" my heart started pounding as excitement made me jittery and anxious.

"Four…" a toothy grin took over my face as I buried my face in my arms to keep myself from releasing a laugh.

"Three…" my body tingled with the need for something to happen, but I shoved that feeling down, forcing my mind to calm down.

"Two…" I bit my lower lip in anticipation.

When the time came for the last number to be said, there was silence. I lifted my head slightly in case it was just a trick to make me leave my hiding place. When I didn't see him where I left him, I stood cautiously only to gasp in complete horror as bile raised in my throat.

Blood- it was *everywhere*! The field was a picture of gold just seconds ago. Now it looked as if a bloody murder took place- *murder*! My heart stopped beating in my chest, air refused to enter my lungs. Fat ugly tears drenched my face until my eyes landed on a pile of bodies. My shallow breath hitched, and my throat began to close. Thrown in a heap as if they were trash, was Aric and my mother.

"This isn't real." My voice cracked. The tears came faster. I took a step back. "This isn't real!" Spinning on my heels, I was prepared to bolt when a chest blocked my path. Following the expanse of the chest, I could only notice one thing- they were *soaked* in blood. My baby brother and mother's *blood*! When I reached the face, my breath hitched in utter terror. "Father?"

"If you speak of this," he started; his cold, emotionless voice coupled with his empty eyes sent a shiver of unadulterated *fear* down my spine. "I'll leave you to die, or I'll kill you too." My body froze.

This isn't real!

He took a step towards me.

This can't be real!

His fingers wrapped around my throat, and he *squeezed*.

"You won't say a *word*!"

"No!" I rasped, shooting up straight in bed.

My wide unfocused eyes frantically scanned the room for anyone- especially my father. My chest heaved painfully as breath wouldn't stay in my lungs. My body- my *heart* just *hurts*! Putting a hand over my chest, I rocked myself back and forth, focusing on breathing.

"It was just a dream," I whispered to myself, tears staining my cheeks. "It was just a dream." *a nightmare caused by a monster.* I curled myself into a tight ball as I lay back down on the cot.

This is all his fault. Aric and my mother's death, being forced to leave without seeing them buried, and now these *nightmares*- all his fault! He caused all of this, and for what? Is he running from someone he wronged? Did he steal something from someone, and now they're trying to get back at him? Did *he* murder someone, and now they're trying to exact revenge?

What did he do?!

"I'll never forgive him," I whispered softly to myself, my breathing finally back under control. "I'll never forgive him," I repeated until I surrendered to the sweet numbness that held me in its grasp. Staring at the wall in front of me with cold, lifeless eyes.

***

I think three hours passed since I woke from my numbness. My limbs were stiff and aching from being forced to lay in a ball for so long. I stood up slowly, giving my legs a good stretch before venturing out of the cabin. I made my way back up the stairs onto the deck of the ship. The moon shone brightly overhead, illuminating the vessel in an ethereal glow. The heavy scent of saltwater ravaged my nostrils, causing it to scrunch up in distaste. Climbing onto the upper deck, I closed the door before dusting off my hands on my dress.

"Is something the matter, madam?" I turned my head only to see a young man- no older than twenty- wielding a broom and a bucket. He was clothed somewhat casually for someone who works for an ex-pirate. A white baggy shirt tucked into a pair of dark brown breeches held up by a belt with a rapier tied to his left hip and a pistol on his right. His dark blonde hair was tied in a low ponytail at the base of his neck, causing the end to barely reach past his shoulder blades.

"What makes you think anything is wrong? Is there something strange about me wanting to enjoy the view of the ocean at night?" He blinked at me, raising a brow before turning his head to look out across the ocean blue.

"No," he simply said, turning back to me with the smallest hint of a grin. "I suppose it's not for passengers who suffer from nightmares."

"What did-?"

"Most of the passengers we transport has them for one reason or another. They find passing the restless night hours standing on the deck, gazing at the ocean helpful. I don't see how you wouldn't gain the same benefits." He shrugged, walking passed me to get back to his duties. I narrowed my eyes at his back before huffing, turning to walk away. "Oh, and try not to inhale too much saltwater! Some of those troubled souls found themselves jumping overboard because of the delusions it brings!" I stopped in my tracks, whirling around, but empty space was all that was left.

"Are ya lookin' fer yer father, missy?" I jumped slightly, twirling around on my heels only to see a shirtless man wearing pants cut to his shins and a jagged dagger tied to the cloth holding them up sitting on the railing, his back towards me.

"Aren't you afraid of falling?" I asked, warily keeping my distance from him.

"Nay, just be a fool who looks out fer danger.." He unsheathed his dagger, tossing it hazardously in the air and catching it with his hands either by the hilt or the blade. "Ye'r father went down to the Captain's quarters nearly an hour ago. He should still be there if ye'r lookin' for him, missy." I scoffed.

"The only reason I'd be looking for him is to push him overboard." A light chuckle left his lips as he threw his dagger higher, catching it mere inches away from landing in his eye.

"I'd be interested in listenin' in on what those two have to say if I were ya missy. Sounded like somethin' important. Might it be the reason ya be on this ship, I wonder?" I glared suspiciously at his back. Is he taunting me? "Ye may want to hurry before the two stop talkin', or would ye rather watch my back some more?" I snorted quickly, walking away from the strange old pirate. I approached Jin's cabin quietly as not to alert them to my presence, but the closer I got to the door, the more I could make out of their conversation.

"… Be a trick?"

"Yes. Your contract was not signed by the person who employed you but under a false name. I can look more into it when we reach Rosesea."

"Why can't ye look now?"

"I don't have the proper resources here, but I can assure you I will fulfill my end of the bargain as long as you fulfill yours." Shuffling of clothing followed.

"Aye, aye, mate. Don't worry 'bout that. I will get ye and the lass there safely. It seems like I have some business to attend to up north."

"I can get you their real name within two days after docking."

"Aye, which dock did ye want me to take ye?"

"Jancliff in Eastrock."

"Aye, right, the small one. I wonder what a politician like ye'r self is goin' to do out in the country- and with a little lass to raise no less. Ye know there's goin' to be plenty of young mates lookin' to take her from ye."

"Jayde does- and will do- as she is told."

"Nay, mate. Ye don't seem to know the young lass's mind."

"I know my own daughter, Captain Jin."

"Nay, ye knows what ye wants to see. What's really there may be somethin' ye can't fathom."

"What can you possibly know about my daughter that I don't?"

"I be an ex-pirate, mate, not a cleanin' boy only good for scrubbin' decks and outhouses. Not even a minute after I met the lass, and she already speaks to me as if I be her father and not ye! I say not even one-word bout ye, and the lass is ready to drown herself. Ye need to watch out for the lass, or else I'll take her to someone who will." I held my breath as the tense atmosphere grew silent. Anticipation filled me the more time passed for my father's response.

"If you think that way when we reach Jancliff, then feel free to do so." My heart jumped into my throat as I took a step back.

So, he really doesn't want me.

Closing my eyes slowly, I took in a deep breath.

"I *will* find out what you did," I whispered, opening my eyes into a hard glare. "Then, I will rest in peace, watching you rot behind bars."

***

A week into the journey, I was no closer to finding out the reason as to why my family was murdered. I did everything I could think of from rummaging through my father's few belongings he got from Jin to asking Jin's crew about what they know. All of my efforts ended in dead ends. Nothing of any value came up. The only thing that I got from my research is that my father is running away from someone, but given I already knew that, it was useless information.

By week two, I began to realize what Jin and that crew member said about the saltwater in the air. From time to time, when I spent a lot of time above deck, I would see glimpses of Aric running around or my mother sitting on the steps knitting. However, I haven't decided if it was from the salty air or lack of sleep, though the latter is more likely.

Since the first night, the nightmares have been getting *worse*. In the beginning, it always seems like a safe haven- a sanctuary- but it always ends the same. It *always* ends in some brutal murder scene, with my father being the only suspect. Just to keep some semblance of sanity, I've only allowed myself to sleep three times in the past seven days- none of them any longer than four hours. For the rest of the time, I hunted for more clues as to what happened that night. However, just like the week before, it yielded no results- just more useless information I already knew.

By the third and final week of the journey, I was more determined and delirious than ever. My hallucinations got to the point where I could feel and speak to the images my mind created as if they were alive. Afraid that I wouldn't be sane enough to keep searching, I went to the last place I thought I would have to go to, the Captain.

"Ye want me to tell ye who killed ye'r family?"

"Yes, you're the last person I can turn to."

"Aye, bein' as there be not many people on my ship."

"Can you help me, Captain Jin?"

"What gives ye the thought I can?"

"You speak with my father in your private meetings- he must have told you something!"

"Nay, he hasn't, lass. I know as much as ye do." He crossed his arms over his chest, fixing me with a stern look. "When was the last time ya slept, lass?"

"Yesterday." His eyes narrowed as he turned, walking around his desk. He opened a drawer and pulled out a pouch tied closed with a thin red string. He tossed the bag to me. I barely was able to move fast enough to catch it.

"Eat that before ye retire tonight. It will help ya sleep through the night."

"What is it?"

"Herbs from Pryland, lass. They calm the mind so ye can sleep without dreams." I examined the pouch, absently wondering how awful I must look to make him so worried.

"Thank you, Captain Jin, I'll be sure to take it tonight." I quietly agreed, keeping my eyes averted to the ground.

"Aye, and if there is somethin' else botherin' ya, come to me."

"Concern sounds strange coming from an ex-pirate Captain." His bellowing laughter filled the cabin.

"Aye, it be true." He grinned crookedly, sitting down in the chair behind his desk. "Go to ye'r quarters; take the herbs, and rest, lass. By the time ye rise, we'll be in the docks of Jancliff." I nodded, repeating my thank you and robotically heading down to my cabin. I don't remember the journey there, but I do remember taking the herbs and my head hitting the stiff pillow on the cot before darkness.

***

The sound of yelling woke me- not a nightmare. My head bolted up, no longer feeling heavy and clouded. Actually, my entire body felt refreshed and rejuvenated. What were those herbs anyway? The sound of more yelling and horns blaring cut off my mental questioning.

Making my way above deck, I was immediately assaulted by the bright sunlight and the sound of seagulls squeaking. When my eyes adjusted, all I could see were the sails of small ships fluttering in the light breeze. The scent of saltwater wasn't as strong as it used to be. Now, I could smell something that I didn't realize I missed until it registered in my brain- dirt.

"Land ho, land lovers!" Captain Jin's voice boomed from the helm of the ship. A broad grin formed on his face when he caught sight of me. "Welcome to Rosesea, Port Jancliff of Eastrock!"

IV

The port of Jancliff was small but crowded. Since Jancliff is a prominent fishing town, it was no surprise to find that there were many stalls set up selling different kinds of seafood- familiar and exotic alike. The stall vendors screamed and shouted, trying to outmatch each other and the blaring horns of the ships coming and going. Other people ranging from fishers to ship passengers to townsfolk bustled through the chaos doing whatever business they came to complete. On the other hand, I stood next to the ramp leading to Captain Jin's ship with my arms crossed, and my attention focused on anything that wasn't my father next to me.

"Thank you again for your generous hospitality." My father said while holding out his hand to shake Captain Jin's. The ex-pirate captain looked down at it before letting out a bellowing laugh knocking his hand out of the way and pulling him into a manly embrace.

"Come on, mate- ye be in Rosesea now! Keep all that civility back in Clearapal with the lot of those bigots! Relax, mate!" He let my father go patting him hard on the back before turning his eyes to me. "I'm sure the little lass here will show ye exactly how to blend in with us savage folk!" He closed the distance between us and holding his arms out in an expectant hug. I smiled, wrapping my arms around him.

"I'm going to miss you, Captain Jin." We pulled back, neither of our smiles leaving our faces.

"Ye make it sound like I be leaving forever, lass."

"Then, when will I see you again? Or better yet, can I stay with you?" A laugh left his lips as he smacked my back gently.

"Nay, lass, not after those two weeks ye spent on my ship hallucinating about that which be dead. Ye be better off a land lover."

"I could learn to be on the sea. Besides, it's not like anyone needs me." His shoulders rumbled as the faintest sound of a chuckle left his lips.

"Ye'll be fine. Ye'r scurvy dog of a father is a good mate underneath all that sluggard talk! Give'em a chance." I rolled my eyes but couldn't help but smile at the insults he threw at my father even though I had no idea what any of them mean. A 'scurvy dog'? 'Sluggard talk'?

"I'll try my best."

"That's the spirit, lass! Now get going before it be gettin' dark-wouldn't want ya swimming with the fishes because ye didn't get to where ye'r goin' in time!" He patted my back once more as I laughed. He allowed a bellow of his own as he turned back around to my father.

"Thank you again, Captain Jin." Said man made an exaggerated swooping bow removing his hat in a lavished sweep of his hand.

"It be my honor to help such a noble family such be ye'r selves." This time when my father held his hand out for him to shake, Jin clasped his own into his. Just as my father went to pull his hand back, Jin held on tighter and pulled him closer, whispering something into his ear. My father's emotionless face never wavered when he nodded slowly, taking out a pouch full of money.

"For your confidentiality and services." Is all he said. Jin raised a brow at the bag before taking it and tucking it away in one of the pouches attached to his belt.

"It be a pleasure, but this sea dog is needed back in the wide-open blue. Until fate sees us together again!" He shouted, making his way back up the ramp to his ship. "Prepare to set sail!"

"Aye, Captain!" a chorus shouted back as the crew members bustled around doing their respective jobs. Jin made his way to the helm of the ship, taking the wheel into his hands. He turned back to us with a crooked grin on his face.

"Take care, land lovers!" A glint filled his eyes as he seemed to remember something. He pulled back his coat and pulled out a rather large sack. "For ye, lass! Try to make it last until ye can get more!" he tossed the bag to me. I caught the mildly heavy sack, nearly dropping it to my surprise. I held the sack close to my chest, a stupid smile plastered on my face.

"Thank you, Captain!" I screamed as loud as I could. Jin smiled, placing two fingers to his forehead before moving them slowly towards me in a farewell. In the next instant, the sails of his ship fell free from their bindings, and the vessel quickly started to gain speed sailing out of the docks.

I watched his ship until it disappeared under the horizon before opening the sack. Inside held a change of clothes consisting of a pair of black riding breeches, a white button-up top, and a couple of riding boots. Also included was a blanket, a pouch filled with money, and some dry food rations.

"We will be heading into town to find transportation to our next destination." My father said, already walking away. I glared at his back, waiting until he was a reasonable distance away before following. Considering I was in a country I've never been to with absolutely no knowledge of it besides the fairytales and ghost stories I've heard, it would be suicide not to follow- even if I *really* didn't want to.

"Even if I ask, I know you're not going to tell me because you're just that much of a psychopathic monster, but where are we going?" As I predicted, my father didn't answer me. He just kept walking as if I hadn't said a word. That's alright though, I didn't want to start a conversation with him. All I want are answers.

We walked for a few minutes until the market square came in view. As I thought, the whole place reeks with the stench of rotten fish, saltwater, and musk I hope is body odor. My face twisted in disgust at the scent. On the other hand, my father just continued walking as if there was nothing wrong. I scowled at his back in mild jealously that he could so easily ignore such revulsion.

Then again, he had plenty of practice ignoring his family for years.

The dark thought swirled in my head until it brought repressed memories to the forefront of my mind. I closed my eyes tightly, forcing them back to where they came from.

"Hello! What can I do you for you, sir, madam?" My eyes opened only to see a man seated on top of a carriage with a piece of straw in his mouth, grinning down at us. He wore a worn hat on his head that served no other purpose but to block the sunlight from his face. He wore traditional coach driver clothing- white baggy shirt, brown breeches, riding boots, and a large coat over it. Judging from the stubbles of hair on his chin, I could only guess he was around my father's age.

"We're looking for transportation to Redmage just west of here. My daughter and I are looking for a new home after my wife died of an illness." Why does it not surprise me that he didn't even think to mention Aric? Though he did seem to catch the driver's sympathy as his eyes softened.

"I'm sorry to hear about your loss." He turned his eyes to me, and they seemed to sadden even more. "A young lady like yourself shouldn't be without their mother so soon."

"It was, indeed, a sudden tragedy." I murmured, lowering my head. Out of the corner of my eye, I could see my father shooting me a nasty glare that I could only smirk at. What does he think I'll do? Tell someone that my family was murdered by an assassin for some mysterious reason that only my father and his bodyguard knows? He would probably drive himself mad like I am just trying to make sense of the whole situation!

"We don't have much money. I had to give up everything I own to pay for my wife's treatment, but I was able to get a little money from a few jobs throughout our travels. I'm not sure if it will be enough for both of us to get to Redmage." The driver seemed to contemplate this while looking at my down casted eyes with blatant pity and, strangely enough, admiration.

"I usually charge six gold pieces per person for going that far out, but I can make a deal with you for the little lady's sake." A smirk covered his face once again when I lifted my chin. "There's plenty of kind folk in Redmage that will make you feel right at home! I've lived there since my parents passed when I was six. I'm sure the townsfolk will care for you as they cared for me." I smiled back at him gratefully. His smile brightened even more before he turned to my father. "How much do you have?"

"I'm afraid I only have eight gold pieces." My father pulled out a small pouch and opened it, showing he, sure enough, only had eight gold coins. He handed over the money to the driver, who weighed it in his hand before pocketing only two and giving the rest back to my father.

"I think only two gold coins will be enough this time. I usually use the rest of the money to pay for hay for the horse, but since we're going to Redmage, it won't matter much." I couldn't help but smile at the pureness radiating from him.

"Thank you so much, sir. You're very kind." He rubbed the back of his head with a nervous grin.

"It's nothing, little lady. I'm just doing what I would want anyone else to do for me." I was about to say more to thank him, but my father grabbed my arm and pushed me towards the carriage door.

"Thank you, sir." The driver raised his brow at my father as he swung the door open and stared at me expectantly.

"Call me, Caiden." He said as an afterthought, a suspicious glint in his eye as he looked between my father and me.

"Thank you, Caiden." My father repeated before he put a hand on my back and none to gently, pushed me to the carriage door. I glared at him before climbing inside. Immediately after, my father climbed in as well. Without saying another word, Caiden snapped the reins, and the carriage lurched forward.

"Don't call yourself Jayde anymore." My father suddenly said, keeping his eyes glued outside the window as if he were looking for someone.

"No."

"Jayde-"

"My mother gave me my name. You've already taken her and my brother away from me- why would I allow you to take away my name too?" he was silent for a while, never once looking at me.

"Your name from now onwards will be Ella Vale. When speaking of me, call me Krish Vale. Our past life was working as farmers in a small town in the north. Your mother passed away due to disease."

"Why does it not surprise me that you didn't include Aric in your little lie? Or do you even remember that he existed?"

"Jayde-"

"I thought my name was Ella, Krish."

"Stop it- now."

"I'll stop when you tell me what you did to cause all of this."

"I told you to leave it alone."

"And I told you I wouldn't until I found out what happened that night." His head snapped towards me with an enraged fire burning behind his eyes. Before I could even react, his hand snapped out and caught my arm in a bruising grip. Pulling me towards him, he allowed a snarl to form on his face.

"I will *not* tell you again, little girl. Drop this subject, or I will leave you in Redmage. Am I clear?" I stared hatefully back at him as he roughly released my arm.

"I hate you."

"When we get to Redmage, don't attract attention to yourself like you did back on the ship." I didn't answer him. I sat in my seat, staring out of the window.

***

After four hours of travel, we finally arrived at Redmage. Caiden pulled the carriage up to the small stables on the outskirts of the town. When the carriage stopped, my father wasted no time in jumping out before Caiden could get the chance to open the door for us.

"Ella, let's go." I stared at my father with blank eyes patiently waiting for Caiden to walk over and help me out of the carriage.

"Well," Caiden started eying my father with distrustful orbs before turning his gentle eyes towards me. "I hope you find a welcoming home here!"

"Thank you for your kindness again." He gave me a crooked smile rubbing the back of his head.

"I told you before, there's no need to thank me." He dropped his hands, placing them in his pockets. He glanced once more at my father before turning his full attention to me. "If you ever need anything, there's a kind old woman who sells bread in the market you can go to. Or, if you ever need another ride somewhere, I come back every few days to make my rounds."

"I will keep that in mind. Thank you, Caiden." My father cut in, placing a hand on my shoulder to steer me away from Caiden. I was about to push away, but he dug his nails into my shoulder warningly. I bit the inside of my cheek to repress the string of unkind words that would surely leave my lips if I opened my mouth.

"Alright, until next time, Mr. Krish, Lady Ella." Caiden glanced at my father before turning around and making his way back to the carriage.

My father immediately turned away, heading towards the center of the town. Once we were out of Caiden's sight, I jerked out of his reach, shooting him a disgusted scowl. He didn't even flinch. He just did as he's always done and ignored me continuing on to the market.

A few minutes later, we made it to the market. As I thought, there aren't many people here- just a few dozen residences. While my father walked ahead of me, I took the time to look around at the people we passed. Unsurprisingly, there are a lot of distinct differences between them and me.

Everyone here was unconditionally *happy*. It's almost as if nothing could ruin their day because they have some form of undying optimism. Even the simplest of actions they do can bring them joy and happiness.

A stark contrast to me.

I am absolutely *miserable*. My father is an insufferable maniac who has done something to completely ruin our family's life, and he won't even tell me *why*. Just to add to the mountain of horror, I will *never* get the chance to see my baby brother or mother again. Compared to these happy people, I'm merely a fatally wounded cat waiting for something to take the pain away.

"This is where the town's representative stays." My father called towards me as we approached a large three-story building settled in the middle of the market square with the words REDMAGE LAW printed over the door. "I'm going to go inside to see if I can't find us a home and a job. Stay out here until I get back, understand?" I didn't even look at him- he's not worth the effort. As always, he didn't care. He just turned around and walked into the building as if I didn't exist.

I glared at the door as it closed behind him. When I heard the click signaling it was securely shut, I turned away and began backtracking my steps to a small stand I saw on our way here. It looked like a bread stand where you can buy fresh bread. Didn't Caiden say that there was a sweet old woman who owns it that I could go to for help? When I saw the stand in my sights a few seconds later, I picked up my pace as an elderly woman stood behind it with a scarf wrapped tightly around her head.

"Hello, little lady." The woman greeted, her brown eyes shining with a light of mischief that made me smile.

"Hello to you as well," I replied, taking a glance around her stand.

"Are you searching for anything in particular?"

"No, I was just wondering if you knew a man by the name of Caiden." Her eyes shined in recognition before they narrowed slightly.

"Yes, I know that young blooded coach driver. What has he done? Has he made ya pay more for your ride than what it was worth?" I raised a brow in surprise. Why would she think someone as sweet and kind as Caiden would do such a thing?

"No, I was only asking because he told me that if I ever needed anything, I could ask the old lady that sells bread in the market for help. I just wanted to make myself acquainted with you before I just come by and ask for things." The woman snorted and began to organize the bread on her stand almost obsessively.

"I don't know who that youngen is calling old, but it ain't me!" She grumbled, finishing up her organizing to her satisfaction.

"It must not be because you're old or anything," I mumbled, picking a loaf of bread and inspecting it. The woman snorted again before opening her mouth to say something, but the giggling of a girl cut her off. Both of us turned our heads to see a little girl- no older than seven- running towards us with red pigtails flopping behind her. A smile was plastered on her face as she clutched a bouquet of sunflowers in her hands.

"Grandmother!" She shouted as she came closer.

"Karlie, where did you run off to this time?" the old woman scolded. The little girl stopped in front of her on the opposite side of the stall of me.

"I was with big brother Caiden!" Karlie excitedly squealed before shoving the flowers in her hands towards the old woman's face. "He brought me flowers from Jancliff!"

"That's nice darling, but don't run off again."

"Okay, grandmother, but you have to take the flowers!" The old woman didn't say anything else, but she took the flowers from the little girl's hands and set them down on the stall. Karlie smiled happily before she noticed my presence. "Hello, stranger! What's your name?"

"My name is… Ella." The name sounded awkward coming from my lips. Is it because I'm claiming it as my own when it isn't?

"Hello, Ella! My name is Karlie!" She grabbed hold of her grandmother's arm, a light shining in her bright brown eyes. "This is my grandmother, Ginger!" I nodded, not really knowing what else to say on the subject. Seriously, what can I say?

"I haven't seen you around here before." I turned my attention back to the old woman- Ginger.

"I just arrived here today."

"Where did you come from?"

"A small town in Clearapal."

"I don't believe that. Nothing is small in that giant place- nor is there anything worth running from if you don't count the backstabbing, bloodthirsty nobles that live there." She mumbled, going back to straightening her bread. I resisted the urge to defend myself in her accusation against nobles, considering that *I* am one, but then I found that I couldn't bring myself to do it. I mean, what have me, my family, or anyone I know done that wasn't with the intent of self-gain? I can't think of a single moment in time that has happened. So, I can't defend myself because there is nothing to protect.

"I guess so." Her eyes lingered on mine as I kept my head down, staring intently at the bread. It's almost as if she *knows* I'm not telling the truth. How would that be possible?

"Well, it's a good thing that you won't be finding any nobles of the sort here in Rosesea."

"Rosesea isn't a place that nobles would like to go to. It's just forests and rocks out here." I mumbled, examining my nails.

"Now, I believe you're from Clearapal- you sound like a native."

"How?"

"There's a lot more to this place then what you've been taught." I raised a brow at her explanation, causing her to sigh in annoyance. She slammed her hands against the stall, making me jump. "Tell me, girl, how many continents are there on this planet?"

"Three."

"And how many of them are inhabited by people?"

"Where is this-?"

"Don't you try to stall, how many?"

"Two," I answered, raising a brow slightly peeved by her sudden mood swing on wanting to talk about geography. What is the point of this?

"Why don't people live on the third continent?"

"I know, I know!" Karlie shouted, holding her hand over her head, eagerly awaiting to be called upon. Glancing down at the little girl, Ginger relented and waved towards her to answer.

"Karlie?"

"It's too far down south! It's too cold for people to live there."

"Do you know what it's called?"

"Pryland!"

"Excellent, Karlie. At least you answer my questions with some excitement." She gave me a sideways look to which I rolled my eyes.

"I would answer your questions with just as much eagerness as the kid if you told me what I'm doing it for."

"To teach."

"What?"

"To teach you that there is more to this world than just people and animals."

"What is that supposed to mean?"

"Think about it, youngen, why do you think our towns and villages are on the outskirts of the forest? Why do you think no one ever ventures into the woods?" My face scrunched up in confusion.

"Wasn't it because of a group of explorers going missing a few decades back?"

"No, it had to do with what's inside."

"Pray tell what that is."

"Beings out of our understanding."

"Beings?" An amused smile stretched across my lips, the urge to laugh irresistible. Really? Does she expect me to believe that?

"Yes." Her eyes darkened as if she read my thoughts, and she was thinking of some way to punish me for them.

"What are we talking about here? Unicorns and ghosts?" Ginger narrowed her eyes before huffing. She turned sideways, folding her arms across her chest, signaling she was finished with the conversation.

"It's pointless trying to educate you with that thought process of yours. I'll try again when you've been here long enough to understand what I say is true." a small giggle left my lips as I pulled out the money pouch Jin gave me taking out a few coins.

"Whatever you say, Granny." She scoffed at the name, closing her eyes.

"It's only one piece of gold."

"Good, because I was only giving you that much anyway," I smirked, placing the money into Karlie's small palm. The little girl put the coin in a container concealed on the other side of the stall.

"Enjoy your bread!" She recited cheerfully with a bright smile. I couldn't help but smile back at the little girl.

A little girl who shares the same laugh as Aric.

"Just as a friendly warning," Ginger started opening her eyes. They seemed to penetrate my very soul as they blazed with a hidden meaning. "Be careful while here. There have been some… questionable folk loitering about in the past few days. It makes me wonder what kind of people Caiden is bringing here."

"What kind of-" a scream nearly burst through my lips as a hand clasped itself roughly on my shoulder. I spun around in fear half expecting to see a man dressed in black ready to kill me, but I only saw my father with a nasty glare plastered on his face.

"I told you to stay in front of the building." Once I was able to calm myself, I scoffed.

"If you haven't noticed, I *am* in front of the building. It's not my fault that you didn't specify how far away I was to stay." His eyes darkened even more as he grabbed my arm in a bruising grip. Before he could drag me away, Ginger spoke, stopping him.

"You should know residents here don't take kindly to people maltreating children." My father slowly turned to her, his glare never wavering.

"My daughter is not a child; she is merely a rebellious teen who needs to learn how to obey."

"I think she is a young lady who you should take your hands off before someone gets the idea that you're not fit to be in charge of her care." My father's jaw tightened, his glare deepened as he released me. I took two steps away from him, rubbing my arm.

"That hurt," I grumbled, glaring daggers at him. He didn't even spare me a glance.

"The representative has given us a home to stay in on the edge of town. Follow right behind me since you aren't able to decide on an appropriate distance yourself." With that, he turned his back and walked away.

I hate him!

Twirling on my heels, I placed a smile on my face.

"It seems my insufferable parent wants to go. I'll come back tomorrow. What time does your stall open?" Ginger glanced passed me before turning her attention back.

"In the middle of the morning hours. Believe it or not, people like to buy bread that early." I nodded, placing my elbows on the stall with a mischievous smile on my face.

"Fascinating! Tell me what type of bread do they buy? Oh, and can you list the ingredients you use to make your bread?"

"Ella!"

"Can you also describe the people that come by?"

"Ella, come now!" My father yelled. The smile on my face widened as I stood up straight, knowing that my father was probably red with rage.

"It seems I should take my leave before my father's head explodes."

"We wouldn't want that now, would we?" Ginger added, the sarcasm laced in her words wasn't missed. I laughed before turning around and walking away, throwing one last wave over my shoulder.

***

As he said, the house is on the edge of town. The small one-story house was made entirely out of brick, giving it the look of a little cottage. It was old, considering there was a musk that betrayed its actual age. Plus, there wasn't even a lock on the door. The only thing keeping intruders out at night is a wooden beam. Hopefully, it wasn't secured in place now.

My father walked straight up to the front door, jostled the handle a little, and forced it open. A huff of dust filled the air as the wind blew through the house knocking off the messy substance from the white sheets that covered the limited amount of furniture in the living room.

At least we won't have to clean the dust off of furniture.

"Go into the other rooms and start taking off the cloth from the furniture. Be sure to count how many bedrooms there are."

"And what are you going to be doing while I do that? Lounge around thinking of more ways to get your family killed?"

"Jayde-"

"I thought my name was Ella."

"I will not tolerate your disobedience any longer!" He screamed, glaring dangerously at me. My eyes snapped to him, watching his every movement in case he decided to attack. "I told you time again to stop speaking about it! If you would listen to me and not draw attention to yourself, then we could actually live here safely without anyone finding out where we are!"

"If you would tell me why people are looking for us, then I would stop bringing it up!" I screamed back just as loud.

"You don't need to know that."

"Yes, I do! If it is the reason why I can no longer see my brother or mother ever again, then I deserve to know! If you would stop being such a cold-hearted, uncaring man, then maybe you can do one good deed in your life and put my mind at ease!" He stared at me with an emotionless expression before turning his back, walking away. My glare deepened as I took a threatening step towards him before screaming at the top of my lungs, "Just because you can't love anything doesn't mean I should have to suffer!" He froze in his movements. Slowly, his head turned towards me- his face ever void of emotion.

"That is none of your concern. I will tell you only once more to drop the subject." My face twisted in disgust. My hand curled into shaky fists, and my eyes stung with unshed tears. He doesn't even *care*!

"I hate you!" I screamed. Turning on my heels, I ran to one of the four doors in the hall next to the front door. He didn't even call out to me as I slammed the door behind me. What do I do? I could leave, but no matter how much I want to, I can't. Despite how awful he is, he's still my father. He's the only family I have left. So, what should I do? Do I tell someone? Who? Maybe the neighbors or Ginger? No- they would definitely throw us out. So, who?

"Uncle Layne." He's always helped me no matter what the problem is. If I write to him about what's happening, then he'll tell me what to do. He might even come to see what's happening. Walking to the covered desk, I slipped the dusty cover off, pulled out a sheet of paper, quill pen, and ink I found inside the top drawer before I began to write.

Once I finished, I left the letter on the desk. I'll deliver it tomorrow. That should give him a week until he responds. Until then, what can I do?

V

Life in Redmage isn't as bad as I thought it was going to be, but it isn't great either. I find here that I am forced to do things that I didn't have to do before like clean clothes, work, wash dishes, work, tend to the yard, and work. Even though it's only been a few days, I still feel as though I've been worked to the bone by that Grandma Ginger at her house making and preparing bread for sell. Honestly, why is making bread so much work?

"You're not grinding it right." A frustrated sigh left my lips. Using more force, I pounded the white doughy substance some more to try and flatten it out like she wanted. Ginger is a complete tyrant and obsessed with how she likes her bread, so I'm finding that I won't be able- or sane- enough to complete the task. "That's still not right."

"How about you do it if I'm not getting it right?" I finally shouted, frustrated. My hands throbbed to a nearly unbearable level with the amount of molding I had to do. How can anyone stand to do this for a living?

"I didn't know you were one to give up, girl."

"I'm not, I just know a tyrant when I see one." A smirk formed on her lips as she moved me aside and began the molding process with practiced ease. Within a few seconds, the bread was molded to perfection and ready to be baked.

"If an old bat like me can do this, then why can't a strong, healthy girl like you?" I rolled my eyes walking out the front door. I sat outside with Karlie by the stand as she spoke and sold bread like a professional.

"If an old bat like you can do it, why do you need a strong, healthy girl to do it for you? What happened to striving for your independence as a capable elderly woman?" I shouted back, leaning back on the porch while lazily watching people walk by. A laugh was the only response I got before the sound of dough being pounded into submission filled the air.

"Why do you and grandmother do that every day?" Karlie suddenly asked, innocent curiosity shining in her eyes. My eyes drifted away from her as I thought about the situation.

"It's just something that we do to make the days seem… better." Her brows knitted together in confusion.

"What's wrong that makes you guys so sad then?"

"Nothing," I rolled my eyes back towards her with a small smile on my face. "It just makes it better." Understanding seemed to dawn on her as she nodded and turned her attention back to the people walking by the stand with a few who stop to inspect and buy bread.

"It's awfully quiet out here," Ginger grunted, walking behind me while wiping her hands off on a towel. Karlie whirled around with a smile on her face as she gestured to the dwindling bread supply laid out on the stand.

"People have been flocking to us today!" She happily yelled. Ginger dragged her eyes along the stall before nodding.

"I see. Good work." The little girl beamed excitedly, turning back around more determined than ever to sell the remaining bread left on the stand. "But it is quiet out here."

"Don't you hear the birds chirping behind the image of rainbows? How about the joyous people singing happy tones while they dance?" She sent me an exasperated look while Karlie just looked confused.

"I don't hear or see any of that, Ella!" She whined, crossing her arms and puffing out her cheeks. I laughed, laying down against the cobblestone porch.

"It's sarcasm, Karlie. One of these days I'm going to teach it to you." She huffed, turning her back to me, still pouting.

"Why don't you teach her a story instead of how to be more like you?"

"What's wrong with teaching her how to be more like me? I'm an awesome person."

"You're a troublemaker, girl. You'll only corrupt my darling granddaughter's young mind." I laughed again before sitting up.

"Alright, I'll tell the little runt a story."

"Yeah, I love stories!" Karlie shouted, excitedly plopping down next to me. I sighed exaggeratedly as I turned away.

"I can't believe I'm actually reciting this dumb story to anyone but my parents," I whispered. Giving my head a good shake, I began the fairytale my parents forced Aric and me to remember since before we knew how to walk. "Once upon a time, in a faraway land lived an explorer by the name Jax. Jax was a highly sought after man because of his bravery, righteousness, and handsome features. Many women wanted to marry him, but Jax was already in love with a beautiful teacher named Malory. The two would do anything for each other- no matter what it may be. So, when Mallory became sick, Jax was prepared to do everything in his power to save her.

Jax searched high and low for someone to cure his wife. One day, while on his travels, he found an elderly doctor living in a tiny town near the sea. Jax begged the doctor to cure his wife, but everything comes at a price.

"I'll cure your wife," the doctor told him, "but in return, I want you to find me a place to live with my wife in peace away from the strife of mortals."

"Where would you want to go that's further away from people then this town?" Jax asked.

"Go into the forest and find my wife and me a place to live out the rest of our days. Once you've returned, I will cure your wife." Jax agreed more determined than ever.

You see, the forest was said to be cursed by spirits that gobble up travelers as they enter. They even sometimes kidnap children from the towns that border the woods and turn them into spirits too. Regardless, Jax began his trek to the forest, for he would do anything to save his beloved Mallory.

Two weeks went by for Jax in the forest, and he still wasn't able to find a safe place for the old doctor and his wife to live. He searched everywhere and even fought off spirits that tried to eat him. Finally, on the last night of the second week, Jax fell to his knees and wept.

"I have failed you!" He cried to the sky as the thought of his beloved filled his mind. It's been far too long for her to still be alive, and the old doctor said he will not cure her until he had returned. "All I want… is to find some way to cure her."

After a while, Jax got to his feet and began to walk back towards the village. As he walked, he noticed small glowing spirits- no different from fireflies- drifting along his pathway. The further he walked, the more glowing spirits appeared until the night sky was alit by their ethereal glow.

"Why do you weep?" A young sprite asked, appearing next to him. Surprised, Jax didn't answer her. The young sprite smiled at him hooking her smaller arm with his. "It's okay now." The sprite said with a smile. "My beautiful queen will help you."

The young sprite led Jax down the glowing path to a giant oak tree shining in the night made alive by the sprites dancing and singing within its depths. Jax became anxious, but the promise of his wife being cured made him continue. When they came to the tree, a magical portal opened and transported them to an enormous castle built out of crystals. Jax stared in awe at the beauty around him before noticing the symbol of two gardenias connected to a bell engraved into a sizeable crystallized set of double doors.

"My queen is waiting for you." A new young sprite said, coming next to them. Jax asked them how the queen would know that he was there, but they merely smiled.

"Our queen knows everything." They both said, pushing open the double doors to reveal a giant throne room.

Vines twisted around the room with blooming flowers covering them. In the middle of the back wall sat a crystal throne elevated by three steps. A third young sprite lay on the steps with their eyes closed as if she were sleeping while a beautiful spirit sat on the throne. Her eyes shined a multitude of colors ranging from dark purple, pink, white, and light blue. Natural bright blue circles shined bellow her eyes as she smiled at Jax. The two sprites giggled in adoration next to him.

"What are you called, young traveler?" The queen asked. Jax told her his name, and she giggled before asking him why he was there. Remembering his wife, Jax fell to his knees and wept with his grief.

"My love is very ill, and I don't have the means to pay for her medicine. The doctor told me that if I can find him a safe place in the forest for him and his wife, then he will heal my love. Please, please show me a place that he can live in peace." The queen smiled at Jax as she thought of his request.

"I cannot help you bring people to my lands, Jax, the traveler. However, I can give you something worth the world in riches, but I can only give it to you if you wish for it." Without wasting any hesitation, Jax shouted his answer.

"With my whole being, I wish it!" The queen laughed and held out her palm to him. In the middle appeared a small ring- the frame made of pure obsidian stone that seemed to hold stars within it. In the middle sat a crystal so pure it contained an eternal light blue luster surrounded in pearls. Jax took the ring from her hand before asking what it is.

"This is a jewel that is used to control those around you. Its power is now connected to your blood- no one else will be able to use it. You can sell it or keep it. What you do with it is up to you." Jax thanked the queen profusely. The queen relaxed on her throne and told her sprites to escort Jax back to his village.

The sprites happily accepted and teleported Jax back home. After he shook off his confusion, Jax headed to his home to see about his wife. When he arrived there, he was shocked to see that Mallory was sitting up in bed as if she was never sick. The old doctor sat next to her mashing together ingredients into a mixing bowl.

"I knew you would be back soon, so I wanted to fulfill my end of our deal before it was too late." The old doctor explained. Jax walked to Mallory and checked her temperature to make sure she was indeed alright. When she felt normal, Jax turned back to the old doctor. He thanked him just as enthusiastically as he did the queen before telling him the truth of his exploration.

"I was not able to find the place of which you asked for, but I was given this jewel by the spirit queen in the forest. This should be enough for the treatment." As Jax explained what the jewel could do, the old doctor became fearful and almost frantic.

"Don't tell anyone you have this!" Jax became confused and offered him the jewel once more, but the old doctor refused. "Don't tell anyone you have that! There is a terrible curse connected to anything created by the spirits." Jax quickly agreed to calm him down. For the rest of the week, the old man worked on curing Mallory while Jax sat close by monitoring her recovery. Neither spoke of the jewel again.

Years passed by, and Mallory held no more traces of sickness in her. Jax and Mallory were content with the life they lived but were even more so when their three sons, Gayle, Kyler, and Jasper, were born. Gayle, the eldest, was a courageous and fearless boy like his father, while Kyler, the middle son, was calm and gentle like his mother. Jasper, the youngest, was a caring, brave boy who longed to be an explorer just like his father. The three boys were inseparable and loved their parents as much as their parents loved them. They were the perfect family that protected each other without a second thought to their own wellbeing, but one day, that changed.

It was on a night when an army of bandits attacked their town. The townspeople did what they could to protect themselves, but nothing seemed to work. The bandits made their way through the village- destroying everything in their path as they went- until they came to the doorstep of the family's home. Gayle led his brother's and mother to safety while Jax stayed behind to fend off the bandits, the jewel given to him years before on his finger.

The bandits demanded that he give them everything he owns or else they would take it by force. Jax stood bravely and, using the power of the jewel, ordered the bandits to leave the village and turn themselves into the guard. Under the jewel's spell, the bandits did as they were told. At last, the town was safe, but the memory of the powerful treasure stayed within the mind of every bandit that witnessed it until they grew mad in their want for it.

Their greed consumed them as they sat in their cells until they fought each other over who would get it. The fighting became so violent that they began to slay each other until only one was left alive. The last bandit escaped from his prison and found his way back to Jax's home. Far too deep in his own madness, the bandit captured and killed Kyler after the boy told him that the jewel he searched for did not exist. Enraged, Jax slew the bandit and carried his son's body back home.

The family mourned over Kyler's death. Days turned to weeks, weeks turned to months, and before long years passed, and the family still had not yet finished morning the loss of their precious member. Stricken with grief, Jax traveled into the forests once again, seeking out the spirit queen he met years ago. When he was brought to her castle this time, he did not have a wish, but a single request he hoped she could complete so his family could heal.

"My beloved son was taken from us because the knowledge of this jewel was told to others. I don't want to lose anyone else over this jewel, but I can't get rid of it either. Though this jewel is the cause my son is now gone, it did save my family from a horrible fate. I don't want you to destroy this jewel, but I want you to hold on to it. Keep it safe and hidden from the eyes of those who would want it for their own greedy purposes. Keep it until someone of my blood has come to claim it. That is all I ask of you, spirit queen." Jax bowed towards the queen, and she smiled.

Taking the jewel from his hands, the queen assured Jax that she will hold on to the jewel. Years went by, and Jax became old and frail. It was on the day his sons became adults that he told them the story of the queen. He told them to never forget about it and to keep the memory of it alive through their children until the day came that they may have to go back to the queen and get it." A sigh left my lips as the final words to the tale were spoken. How many times have I recited that dumb fairytale?

"That was amazing, Ella!" Karlie gushed in excitement, clapping her hands together. I rolled my eyes and leaned back against the porch.

"It's just a silly fairytale, Karlie." I laughed. The sound of a rolling pin hitting a hardwood floor created a jolt of fear to run through my body, causing an involuntary twitch. Straining my neck, the sight of Ginger staring wide-eyed at me filled my vision. I narrowed my eyes in confusion. "What's wrong with you? You nearly scared me half to death!"

"Karlie, get inside."

"Why, grandmother?"

"The stall is closing for the rest of the day. Get inside." Karlie didn't question her anymore, opting to pack up the remaining bread on the stall and scramble inside the house. I stood up, raising a confused brow at the old woman.

"Did something happen that I should know about?" Ginger merely glanced at me before shutting the door in my face.

My jaw dropped at the blatant display of rudeness before scoffing and turning around, heading home. Obviously, something is going on with the grandma, but it's not like I can do anything about it. Another sigh broke through my lips as I made my way through the darkening town heading home.

After a few minutes, I made it. As I walked inside, a war cry filled my ears. Without even thinking about it, I fell to the floor, a brush of wind blowing my hair over my face. Trying to catch my breath, I snapped my head up only to see my father standing before me. His eyes were wide open like he was scared; his hands shook as they held a broom in a steel grip. Did he just swing that at me?

"Jayde," he whispered, stumbling back.

The broom hit the floor with a deafening clank as he collapsed onto the couch. His chest heaved as he leaned forward against his knees, burying his face into his hands. A shaky breath left his lips before he went still.

What just happened?

Slowly, I stood from the floor.

"Come home sooner." His voice startled me before what he said registered in my mind.

"Why?"

"Do as I say, Jayde." He snapped quickly.

"If you're not going to tell me why, then I say no."

"Either do as I say or do as you please alone." Anger boiled within me.

"I've been alone since the night my mother and brother were taken from me! You don't even care that they're gone!" I screamed. He shot to his feet and took a warning step towards me, a crazed look in his eyes.

"Jayde!"

"Have you ever loved us? Can you honestly stand here and tell me that you actually-"

"You know nothing!" He screamed. "My family is all I ever had! Everything I did- every little decision I made was so that my family was not put into harm's way!"

"You're a liar and a selfish fool! You made the decision that cost mother and Aric's life! You made the decision that caused us to run away from our home, and for what? For some secret, you refuse to tell me?" Tears streamed down my face, my breath coming out in strained pants.

"Jayde-"

"You don't care that they died because of you!" Silence. His face went completely blank- all the frenzied fear and pure panic in his eyes vanished.

His body was stone still. His back straight raising him to his full height. The ominous chill in the air surrounding him sent a shock of fear down my spine. Without my knowledge, I took a step away from him.

"All my fault." He whispered so low I wouldn't have heard him if I weren't watching him. "All my… fault!" He bellowed in a gut-busting laugh. My eyes widened in shock. I stumbled away from him until my back hit the wall. I watched in utter horror as he threw his head back and laughed uncontrollably to the point he was gasping for air. He just kept *laughing*.

"You're a sick old man!" I screamed, bolting down the hall to my room. I slammed the door behind me, terrified. In my panic, I shoved my wardrobe in front of the door, along with my dresser.

His laughter still rung throughout the little cottage escalating my fear until it became increasingly hard to breathe. Placing a hand over my heart, I focused on breathing taking small steps backward. When the back of my knees hit the edge of the bed, I allowed myself to fall back onto the bed and curl up into a ball. It was only then that I allowed myself to cry- *really* cry. As the glow of the moonlight lit up my little room, I know this is going to be another sleepless night. I could *feel* the nightmares clawing at the edges of my consciousness, threatening to consume me whole in their dark depths. Still, the piercing echo of my father's crazed laughter from the other side of my door did the nightmare's job for them.

VI

"Why do you want to know where a doctor is, girl?" Ginger asked me as she laid out bread on the stall. I rolled my eyes and crossed my arms, a small frown playing on my lips.

"Can you just tell me already, grandma? I have an urgent need for one." She made a sound in the back of her throat, purposefully taking her time in setting out the bread now.

"I feel the need to tell you that the doctor of this town doesn't know a thing about unborn babies." My cheeks blushed red at her implications, and my jaw dropped.

"I don't need a doctor for that, you perverted old woman!" I hissed. She merely let out an amused chuckle as she dusted her hands off after placing the last roll of bread in its place.

"If that's the case, then tell me what you need a doctor for. Either that or I could guess something else a little louder." I glared at the demented devil woman, knowing I had no choice but to give in to her request. I wouldn't want a black mark on my reputation just because some grandma craved answers.

"I need a doctor to help my father." Her eyebrows raised in interests as she stood up a little straighter.

"What happened to him?"

"He's insane. Last night we got into a fight about… what happened to my mother and he completely lost it. He just started laughing like a maniac. When I woke up this morning, he was *still* laughing. I had to climb out of my window just to get here in fear he would try to kill me or something." Ginger nodded her head in understanding before craning her neck towards the house.

"Karlie, come watch the stall while I take the brat to get the doctor for her crazy father!"

"Yes, grandmother!" A dark blush dusted over my cheeks as I glared at the old wench. Did she really have to yell that out so loud?

"Shall we go now, Ella?" Even though there's a smile on her face, I could see the shine of mischief just below the surface.

She did yell that out on purpose!

"I don't like you, old woman."

"Neither do I like you, foolish little girl." I scoffed as she began to lead the way down the street, pass the representative's office building. We walked for a while until the crowds of people started to thicken. As I looked around, I noticed an explosion of stalls and merchants shouting into the masses.

"Is this the main market of Redmage?"

"What does it look like?" I glared at the back of the insufferable woman's head, wishing I could chuck a pebble at it. It wouldn't hurt her much, right?

"Why isn't your stall here then?"

"Why are you so engrossed in my business?" She hummed amusedly. My eyes narrowed into slits.

"You're doing this on purpose, aren't you?"

"I don't know what you mean. I just speak the truth, girl." I grunted, rolling my eyes.

"Sure you do, you vial old woman."

"It breaks my heart that this younger generation has no respect for their elders. What is this world coming to?"

"Stop being so dramatic."

"That reminds me, where did you hear that story you told Karlie?"

"Now who's in other people's business?"

"It's not *your* business unless the story is yours."

"Technically, the story is my family's; therefore, it is my business." A soft hum left her lips as she mumbled something unintelligible.

"Do you know what it means?"

"What are you rambling on about now?"

"Most stories like that have hidden meaning to them. Sometimes that meaning might just be something that can save your life one day."

"It's just a story- there's nothing special about it."

"Whatever you say, little girl."

"Why are you-?"

"Is that my sweet Ginger, I hear?" A man shouted from the steps of a large clean building I didn't realize we were in front of. A creepy smile stretched across Ginger's lips as she strolled inside.

"Are you still trying to sweet-talk me, you old fool?" Bile rose up in my throat as I twisted my face in repulsion.

Am I *really* going to have to sit in a room and listen to two old people flirt with each other? I don't even like it when people my own age flirt! Reluctantly, I followed the two inside of the building. Immediately, the scent of disinfectants and flowers assaulted my nose, causing a slight headache. Ginger sat in one of two chairs situated behind a large desk. The old man sat behind it, pushing his circular glasses on the bridge of his nose. His thick black hair was sleeked back, almost giving off a polished shine in the sunlight. A flirtatious smile was on his face as he eyed Ginger, who was pretending not to notice.

I'm going to be sick.

"I'll stop when you let me take you out to a nice picnic by the lake. We could enjoy a romantic sunset together."

"Oh, stop it, you old flirt! I have a granddaughter to care for- I just simply don't have time for that."

"Then bring her too! I love that little ball of energy almost as much as I love her grandmother."

"You do realize if someone came in here with a health issue, they would be dead by the time you two got your eyes off of each other?" I butted in cutting off whatever remark the old woman was about to reply with. I swallowed hard, trying to keep the bile down. Nearly lost it there for a second.

"Oh yes, excuse me, ma'am, I just get a little distracted when-"

"Yeah, yeah a pretty lady like the old woman here comes into your office, I get it. I just came to see if you can help my mentally ill father, then I'll let the two of you get back to your romance." A chuckle left his lips as he leaned back, relaxing.

"You sound just like Gingersnaps here." He laughed before motioning me to sit in the chair next to Ginger. I grunted, taking the offered seat. "My name is Doctor Patrick. I am a certified physician in many different medical fields. Now, tell me what your father's ailments are so we can see if I can loan you my assistance." He said, picking up a notebook and a pen from his desk, a small smile ever-present on his face.

"He's laughing for some reason. He started last night, and he was still laughing when I left this morning. Even when I came home last night, he was acting violently."

"How so?"

"He tried to knock my head off with a broomstick when I came home."

"Hmm, has your father been a part of any type of war?"

"No."

"A tragic accident?"

"Well, my mother died a few months ago. He hasn't mourned her death once, but that's because he has no soul." The smile grew on his face as he jotted down some notes.

"Is there anything else I should know about his condition besides excessive laughter, violent behavior, and soullessness?"

"No."

"In that case, I'll head right over and see what I can do to help. Maybe I can help your father get a soul." He winked at me placing his pen back on his desk. He stood opening one of his desk drawers and pulling out a doctor's bag. Slipping his note pad inside, he picked up the bag and motioned for us to rise as well. "If you would lead the way, I can get started."

"Of course."

***

A few minutes of walking in agony of having to hear the kissy faces the love doctor and the insufferable old woman made towards each other, we made it to the cottage. The sounds of my father's laughing could still be heard from behind the door, making Patrick raise a brow.

"Excessive laughter even now. That's quite interesting."

"Can you make him stop? The only thing I can think of is hitting him over the head with a rock." Patrick let out a small chuckle before pushing open the door.

"I will not be doing that to your father. Come back at sundown. I'm sure your father will be better by then. If necessary, I will come again tomorrow to continue treatment."

"Thank you, Doctor Patrick."

"You're welcome, dear." He gave me an encouraging smile before closing the door behind him.

"Don't worry about your father, little girl."

"Who said I was?" She turned away, letting out a low chuckle.

"Fine, come back with me to the stall. I've left Karlie there alone for too long already." She called over her shoulder, walking away.

"So, you're just going to assume I'll follow you?" I asked speed walking until I was in step with her.

"You are, aren't you?" I rolled my eyes, turning my gaze to look straight ahead. A comfortable silence befell us as we made the short trek back to the stall. A few minutes later, the small stand was in our sights along with Karlie standing behind it, looking as bored as ever. When she spotted us, her eyes lit up.

"Grandma, Ella!" She cried with a smile stretching across her face.

"What have you been doing while we've been gone, little one?" Ginger softly questioned, coming to a stop beside the girl. The little girl nearly exploded with excitement. She ducked her head under the stall coming up a few seconds later, wielding a jar filled to the brim with gold and silver coins.

"I got a lot of money! I had to restock the supplies twice!" she squealed, shaking the jar in utter bliss. Ginger nodded in acceptance before patting the little girl on the head.

"That's a good girl." Karlie's grin widened as she bent back down and placed the jar back into its place.

"You should leave her here more often if she's making this much money." I teased, walking to the porch and plopping down. Ginger shot me a look from the corner of her eye as she walked past me and entered the house.

"If I were to do that, I think you'd be more worried about the girl than me." She walked back outside and lowered herself down next to me. Her body seemed to shrink as her shoulders slumped, and her head lowered slightly to the point her chin was almost resting against her collar bone.

"What can I say? I guess I have a soft spot for kids." A grunt left her throat.

"Did you have a sibling before?"

"What?"

"From the way you become so protective of my granddaughter, I would assume you've had one before, but I haven't heard you or you father mention one." I allowed my eyes to wander away to stare at something far away in the distance.

"I… did have a little brother," I whispered softly.

"Oh? Where is he?"

"He's… not alive." Tears stung the back of my eyes, but I used every fiber of my being to hold them back.

"What happened to him?"

"He was… killed when he was younger."

"Was it murder?" A shaky sigh left my lips as I closed my eyes.

"No. He… died of illness. It was quick, at least." A thoughtful hum rumbled in her chest as she turned her gaze to stare ahead.

"What was his name?"

"Aric."

"I'll be sure to say a prayer for him then."

"Thank you…" I whispered almost inaudible, allowing my eyes to open halfway.

"Do you remember what he was-?"

"Do you mind not talking about him?" I snapped a little harsher than I meant to. "He died a few years ago, but the scars of his death still haven't faded." She nodded slightly and turned her eyes back forward.

"How about I tell you a few stories about Rosesea?"

"Do they have something to do with fairies and other creatures that don't exist?" She cracked a smile allowing her eyes to lazily drag to me.

"They do because they're real."

"No, no, they aren't."

"You may believe what you want, but it won't change that they are real."

"Maybe in your delusional mind, but in reality, they are fake."

"Are you trying to say that every single person that lives in Rosesea is delusional?"

"Maybe it's something in the water." She laughed.

"That sharp tongue of yours can be a valuable asset, but you should learn to control it in situations where it can get you hurt." I laughed, turning my gaze in front of me, half paying attention to who crossed my line of sight.

"Whatever you say, old woman-" My heart stopped. The breath entering my lungs burned while tears seared my wide eyes.

"Ella?"

"No..." I whispered before immediately, slamming my back against the stall concealing myself. Ginger and Karlie both gave me startled and bewildered looks as if I had gone crazy- not too far from the truth.

"Ella, what's going on?"

"He's here..." I whispered, tears welling up in my eyes. This isn't fear. This is utter *terror*.

"Who's here?"

"I thought he was dead..."

"Ella," Ginger placed both her hands on either side of my head. She looked me straight in the eye, her face deathly serious. "Who is here? What has you so afraid, girl?"

"The man walking across the street... he killed them... he murdered them." When her brow rose, a bubble of frustration and utter panic filled me. I clasped her shoulders in my hands and shook her slightly. "He is here! The man who murdered my little brother and mother is here! I thought he was dead- I thought my father killed him! He found us- he's going to murder all of us!" I shrieked in a high-pitched whisper I knew he couldn't hear from across the street.

"I thought your mother and brother died of disease years ago?"

"No! Those were lies my father made me tell, or else he was going to leave me to die! That *murderer* took my mother and brother away from me because of something my father did! He won't tell me what he did or why this assassin is after us!" My eyes went even larger. My hands flew to my mouth in horror.

"Ella, what is it?"

"He's heading in the direction of the house... he's heading to my house!" I screeched, flying to my feet. Not only is my father there but also Patrick- an *innocent* man who has *nothing* to do with this.

I have to do something to save them!

Lithe wrinkled hands gripped my shoulders and shoved me back down to my knees.

"Ella, breathe, and calm down."

"Let me go- I have to do something!" I hollered, peeling her hands off of my shoulders. Just as quickly, she took hold of my wrist.

"What are you expecting to do by going there?"

"Something more than just sitting here cowering in fear!" Her mouth opened to say something else, but I snatched my arm out of her grip and took off before she could grab me again. "Get the guard and bring them to my house!" I shouted over my shoulder as I continued to run.

***

The moment I got back home, my feet took me straight to my bedroom window. Silently, I climbed inside and scanned the room for any signs of the assassin. When I didn't find any, I moved towards the still barricaded door and began to move the furniture from in front of it as quietly as I possibly could. When I was done, I cracked the door enough to peer out into the small hall. When I didn't see anything, I slipped out into the hallway before immediately slamming my back against the wall next to the corner that blocked my view from the living room. Soft, inaudible mumbles could be heard from the room. I inched closer to listen clearer.

"...else?"

"All of you... every last one of you... all of you are going to burn... you and the bastard that hired you... how did I not see the signs?" My father's voice mumbled in a maniac tone. Taking a deep breath, I peeked around the corner only to snap back around, a single tear falling down my cheek.

In a bloody mess on the floor lay Patrick. He was face down in a pool of his own blood in the middle of the living room floor as if he were a spur of the moment kill and nothing more than trash now. My father was on his knees beside Patrick's body with an eerie grin on his face as he continued to mumble.

Who is he talking about? They must be the ones that caused all of this!

"I will not ask you again, is your daughter dead or alive? I won't kill you if you tell me."

"That rotten snake-"

"I grow tired of your insolent ramblings. Tell me where the girl is."

"Both of you are going to burn-" a sigh was heard from the assassin. In the next second, a sickening sound was heard. The sound of thick liquid sloushing, followed by gurgling sounds before a body hit the floor.

A shaky breath left my lips as I squeezed my eyes shut.

I'm alone now…

Heavy footsteps heading towards the backdoor echoed through my ears. Slowly my eyes opened, and I took a silent deep breath. Inching around the corner, I tiptoed towards the broom lying on the ground by the door from where my father dropped it yesterday. My eyes never left the back of the assassin as he continued to make his way to the back door. The moment my fingers wrapped around the broom, my heart pounding in my chest, I snatched it up, releasing a battle cry as I lunged at the assassin. Almost as if he knew I was coming at him, he spun around and grabbed the broom in a sturdy grip halting me in my tracks.

"There you are." My eyes widened in fear as he snatched the broom from my grip and sliced at me with the bloody dagger in his hands.

I barely was able to jerk backward out of the way in time. He grunted in annoyance and spin kicked me in my abdomen, sending me flying to the ground, sliding to a halt when my back hit the front door. Before I could regain my breath, the assassin wrapped his fingers around my throat and lifted me from the ground. Air was being kept from me by his tight grip causing black spots to dance around my vision. I clawed desperately against his hand, trying to get it off of me while gasping for precious air, but nothing worked.

"To give you peace in the afterlife," he whispered emotionlessly, "I will tell you that you were killed by the assassin Hawk." A tear slid down my cheek as he held the knife over his head.

I don't want to die here!

Using the last of my fading strength, I kicked my foot out. The pained moan and the feeling of air rushing back to my lungs as his grip released me told me I hit the mark. Gasping and sputtering, I saw from the corner of my eye as he clutched at the space between his legs in agony. A feeling of complete satisfaction overwhelmed me as I struggled to stand, towering over the man who murdered my family.

"For the record," I spat still breathless, picking up the knife he dropped after my attack. "You were just taken down by a seventeen-year-old girl name Jayde." I raised the blade above my head, using both hands prepared to complete the deed. "This is for my family." I shoved the knife downwards.

He rolled out of the way and kicked me in the stomach again. I fell to the ground in pain. Before he could get his hands on the knife, the backdoor was kicked in. A large group of cloaked people wearing face masks and hoods rushed into the room, lunging for Hawk. Hawk quickly rolled to his feet and sliced at the first masked person who jumped for him, slitting their throat.

What am I doing watching this? Run idiot!

Without any further hesitation, I scrambled to my feet and took off through the back door. One of the cloaked men saw and tried to stop me, but Hawk got in his way as he tried to chase after me.

"Jayde, wait!" The man shouted. "We can help you!" I didn't stop. I kept running across the yard into the thick cluster of trees. Where I was headed wasn't vital. As long as I'm far away from that house- far away from *death*, I will be okay. I will be okay, right?

VII

My feet ached as I sat in the small wagon filled with hay. The entire carriage rocked as it steadily made its way to Fallbell- a slightly bigger village than Redmage about three miles away. My scraped and bloodied knees were clutched to my chest as my head stayed buried between them. Tears continuously fell down my cheeks as the carriage continued to rock, trying to send me to the nightmares lurking just on the outskirts of my consciousness.

Since the night Hawk came and took my father's life- since the night, I saw his *face*- my nightmares have gotten *worse*. None of them had a happy beginning anymore. All of them were filled with the death of my mother, brother, and now, my father. It always started with some kind of torture scene. My brother, mother, father, and I are still tied in a circle to a chair with my father laughing in the middle and refusing to answer Hawk's questions. Each time he wouldn't answer five questions, Hawk would kill one of us, always starting with my brother. *Always*. He would continue on with my mother, then eventually, my father, and ending off with me *every single time*. Every time, I would wake up choking on my tears and flailing my arms, trying to fight him off.

Before, when we were on the ship with Captain Jin, I thought I was afraid. Now, I know what fear really is. I'm not scared, I'm *petrified*.

Everywhere I turn- everywhere I look, I feel my heart racing. My mind swirling with images of Hawk standing, covered in the blood of my family, with a knife in his hand ready to come after me. When I close my eyes to ward off the hallucinations, I just find nightmares of the dead bodies of my family.

Sometimes, when it really gets bad, I find myself rooted to the ground, held completely still with fear. The feeling of powerful fingers circling around my throat would make my breath come out in painful gasps. My heart would pound against my ribs, words never once leaving my lips. Then all at once, it would just end as if nothing had happened. I would just be left on the ground in the wake of the events sputtering and crying. Is this what I have to look forward to for the rest of my life? Running in fear of this assassin and succumbing to the strangling hold of my fear whenever it decides to come up?

"I just want to know why this is happening…" I whispered to myself as the tears fell faster.

"Whoa, whoa!" The old man driving the carriage called out as the carriage came to a slow halt. I lifted my head slightly to see we had stopped at a semi-crowded stable. The old man turned around and grinned his yellow teeth at me. "We've arrived miss. Sorry if the ride was uncomfortable for ya." He laughed, hopping off the driver's seat and walking around back.

He unlatched the back of the carriage, allowing me to climb down without trouble. Slowly, I crawled to the edge, and, with the kind man's help, I jumped out. I kept my head down so I could wipe my tears away before he could see them. Despite my efforts, he did.

"Are ya sure you'll be alright by yourself? I could give you a place to stay at my home for a few days. My wife could use the help around the house even though she will never admit it." I took a deep breath and shook my head, lifting my eyes to meet his honey-colored ones.

"I'll be fine, I have an aunt who lives here, though I will probably leave here to stay with my grandparents in a nearby town soon. Thank you for your kindness." I gave a weak smile. A small frown found its way to his lips before it was replaced by a half-smile.

"Very well then, I'll see ya around town as long as you stay here. Good luck, little lady!" He saluted me. A sincere grin spread across my lips, and I waved at him before walking away through the crowded streets.

I don't know how long I've been walking just watching numbly as people passed me by going about their day. It's almost like they had no idea that someone marked for death was walking among them waiting for the day a paid assassin comes to take their life away. It just makes me wonder, *is this what's happening back in Clearapal?* It's a sickening thought, but I know nothing has changed even after the news of my family's massacre got out.

Sure, people probably went to the funeral. Some people may have shed a tear or two, but the next day after that, every noble on the continent were competing to take my family's place as the most loved and adored family in the world. After all, nothing means more than power to a noble. The only person I can possibly think of who may still be mourning for my 'death' would be Rose. She may not be crying in public due to her parents not wanting that dark mark on their reputation, but on the inside, she could be. At least, that's what I like to think. We've been best friends since we were barely able to speak. If she were supposedly dead, I would mourn her for the rest of my life, *but would she do the same thing*?

"I wonder what you're doing right now, Rose?" I thought out loud, lowering my gaze to look at my dirtied and ruined shoes. A sigh left my lips as I continued to walk. "What was the reason that all of this happened?" A tear rolled down my cheek.

"Are you okay, miss?" My feet stopped moving. I lifted my head to see a middle-aged man with a frizzy beard and a muscular build standing before me. He wore a heavy black apron that signified that he must be a blacksmith.

"Yes, I'm just… wandering."

"Don't cha have a place to stay?"

"No."

"People looking for ya?"

"No."

"Well, do ya have any money to pay for a place?"

"No." He grunted, rubbing the back of his neck, trying to think of something to say.

"In that case… I may have something for ya to do, as long as ya don't burn yourself." He mumbled as an afterthought. I brought my eyes to look into his and forced a small polite smile.

"That's okay, I don't think I'm cut out to be an apprentice to a blacksmith. Thank you for the offer, sir." Before he could say anything else, I walked away, no set destination in mind as I just wandered.

Hours went by, and I have already walked the length of the entire village. Now, all I can do is walk through the different pathways with my head lowered so no one will bother me. For a long time, no one did, but in the long run, someone with to kind of a heart did. It just so happened to be a young woman in front of a little shop with a carving of two needles and yarn above the door.

"Are you alright?" She asked me as I was walking by. I stopped, turning towards her to see her watching me with concern in her eyes.

"I'm fine," I called back prepared to leave.

"You seem lost; do you need help getting somewhere?" I stopped once again and turned to ultimately face her.

"I'm not heading anywhere in particular."

"Don't you live here?"

"I'm not from around here."

"Then you don't have a place to stay then?"

"No." A look passed over her eyes as she glanced back at her shop for a moment before back to me.

"I think I might have a place for you to stay… but you'll have to work in the shop. My mother-in-law wouldn't like that I'm giving away a place to stay for free." I opened my mouth to decline- to tell her I wasn't good at sewing, but she seemed to see that in my eyes. "Don't worry if you're not good at it. I can teach you how to sew. You'll be a master at it in no time." She smiled kindly and held out a hand to me.

I stared at her outstretched hand for a minute before letting out a deep sigh. Taking the few steps forward to close the distance between us, I placed my hand in hers.

"I guess I can stay for a little while." Her face lit up in happiness as she gave my hand a slight squeeze. She tugged my arm gently towards the front door of the shop while smiling sweetly.

"You'll fit in just fine here, darling." She pushed the door open and allowed me to walk in first.

I stepped inside the spacious shop filled with colorful and multi-patterned cloths with a few manikins dotted around the space near the checkout counter. Behind the desk laid a door that most likely led to the back where the seamstresses spin the cloth into clothing.

"Where do you live?" I asked, turning around just as she closed the door. The bright smile never left her face as she walked towards me and tucked my arm into hers, leading the way to the door behind the counter.

"My house is above the shop. My husband is a carpenter, so his shop is on the other side. He travels quite a bit for his work, so he won't be here for most of the time." She explained in a single breath as she pushed opened the door.

The first thing that came to my field of vision was rows upon rows of clothes and textiles lining the walls. In the middle of the room sat large working stations with models set up next to each of the three tables. One of the marionettes wore an elegant dress that looked fit to be worn to a ball.

"Who made that?" The lady followed my gaze, and her eyes lit up in excitement.

"My mother-in-law made that one. She's very talented! "

"Do you sew?"

"Yes, but all of my work is still in progress." A light seemed to blaze to life in her head.

She let go of me and made her way over to one of the empty workstations. She bent down, grabbing something before standing up straight with a white box in her hands. She walked back over to me with a smile on her face.

"I do have this ready, though. A lady from Clearapal ordered this a few months ago, but she canceled her order yesterday. I was going to put it on display, but I think you need it more." A nervous smile found its way to her lips as she mentioned my torn and ruined clothes. I didn't even bother to glance down at myself as I gratefully took the box from her hands and smiled.

"Thank you, ma'am." Her eyes suddenly widened as a hand flew to her cheek in utter mortification.

"Did I not tell you my name yet? Oh, I am so sorry!" She exclaimed, putting both of her hands to her cheeks and shaking her head in shame before she placed a smile on her face and holding out her hand to me. "My name is Leona Mayflower, what is yours?"

"Jayde… Jayde Henryk." I whispered almost as if it was a foreign word on my tongue. Has it really been that long since I have said my real name?

"That's a wonderful name! Your parents chose a beautiful name for a beautiful girl."

"Thank you…"

"Where are they now? Were you separated? Where you attacked?" My eyes softened at the sincere concern in her voice. When was the last time I've heard someone sound so concerned about me before?

"My parents… are dead… along with my little brother. They were murdered by… some thugs who wanted to steal from our home. I was barely able to escape with my life to get the guard, but… by the time we got back… the thugs had already gone, and my family was…" the last few words stuck in my throat. She seemed to see this, and her eyes sadden as she closed the distance to me and wrapped her arms around my neck.

"I'm so sorry you had to go through something like that." She whispered into my hair. Tears pricked at the corners of my eyes, but I forced them back.

"Thank you… Miss Leona." She gave me a tight squeeze as I felt a wet drop fall on my head. I took a deep, shaky breath as she pulled away and wiped at her eyes, placing a comforting smile on her face.

"It's going to be okay now. As long as you stay here, you won't be alone, I promise." A sincere smile made its way to my lips as I nodded.

"Okay."

***

For the next few weeks, life with Leona and her husband, Aaron, have been some of the best memories I could possibly ask for since the day of my family's massacre. Leona and her mother-in-law, Emily, have taught me everything they can about sewing and cutting fabric to make clothing. Just like Leona said, I absolutely sucked at first, but over the time of their lessons, my skills went to non-existent to slightly above mediocre. Now, just three weeks into my training, I can sew the full outfit I used to wear back in Clearapal. As a matter of fact, I can make my own clothes and wear them as long as I paid for the materials I used.

My clothes are like they used to be, but now I added in an all-black cloak to wear over the dark green dress and opaque brown tights. I had to buy a pair of black riding boots from the store down the street, but they weren't too expensive considering the man who worked there was very kind and sympathetic to my story after Leona told basically the entire town. Now, I get random gifts and awkward letters telling me how much the people of the city love and adore me. However, despite the awkwardness and weird encounters with the residences, I wouldn't want life any other way.

I love every aspect of the life I am now able to live. Everything is peaceful, and I have even been able to get through a full night of sleep a couple times without nightmares. Of course, I still think about my family. Of course, I still have night terrors and the sudden attacks of paralyzing fear, but now they aren't as frequent or severe. It's like I'm slowly getting used to living normally. Maybe, just maybe, I will be able to find peace. Not happiness, but contentment.

***

"Do you have the order for that dress ready yet, Jayde?" Leona called to me from the front. I sat at my working station, putting the finishing touches on the dress she spoke of before cutting the thread and taking a step back to assess my work.

"It's finished!" I shouted back, carefully taking the dress off of the manikin and folding it neatly within a white box. Picking up the large box, I carried it to the counter and plopped it down with a slight huff.

"You remembered to put it in the box this time, good job." Leona teased jotting down notes about the dress on a piece of paper before sticking it on top of the box. "The postman will be by today to pick it up. Just make sure when he comes, he doesn't forget to drop off the payment, okay, Jayde?" I nodded, allowing a small smile to form on my lips.

"You just make sure to not make lovey-dovey eyes at him like last time." She rolled her eyes as an embarrassed blush formed on her cheeks.

"I was not giving him 'lovey-dovey' eyes! He had a massive hole in his shirt, and I was trying to find a way to tell him about it, and you got the wrong idea! I swear, Aaron still isn't over it even after I explained it to him." I laughed, walking back into the back room, pulling off a few pieces of cloth from the wall and bringing them to the front.

I placed them up on their displays neatly. As I was straightening the final one, a nagging feeling told me to look outside. Curious, I lifted my head, and my heart dropped. My throat felt like a desert as my body froze in place.

Standing right outside of the shop was Hawk. He was talking to the man who ran the general store right next door. They seemed to be having a sad conversation. The sweet man listened with his eyes downcast and spoke softly. When he turned his head towards me and raised his hand, pointing his finger at the shop, my mind went blank. Hawk turned his head as well to see what the man was looking to. When our eyes connected, I went completely numb.

Run!

Without wasting a second, I turned on my heels and bolted towards the back door.

"Jayde?" Leona called after me. I ignored her and busted through the workroom door going straight through towards the other door that leads to Aaron's carpenter shop.

I ran straight through his shop's front door and up the street towards the stable.

Please, oh please don't let him find out I was staying with them! My mind cried as I kept running.

My breath was ragged when the sight of the stables came into view. A burst of energy sent me surging forward towards a horse that was already prepared to ride. I slammed my body against the post it was tied to, immediately forcing my shaking hands to untie the reigns holding him hostage.

"Come on, come on!" my hands shook manically as I tried my best to steady them to untie the reigns. A scream ripped through my throat as a bullet embedded itself into the post next to my head. Allowing a quick glance back, the sight of Hawk sprinting full speed towards me with a pistol in his hands caused my heart to stop beating. Whirling around, I yanked on the reigns hard, forcing it out of its knot.

Without wasting a second, I swung my body into the saddle. As the horse spurred forward, another bullet rushed past my head, causing a scream to erupt from my throat. I lowered my torso to the point my body nearly disappeared within the horse's mane. The sound of another gunshot going off fueled my curiosity enough to make me turn my head. My heart sunk into my stomach at the sight of the kind old man who brought me to this peaceful little town lying dead in the middle of the stables as Hawk watched me. I snapped my head back around and urged the horse faster, never letting up even when we entered the thick line of trees that connected Fallbell with Redmage.

"Please don't slow down," I whispered desperately to the horse as tears pricked at the corner of my eyes. The horse grunted in disapproval at me but never stopped running, expertly dodging trees. I didn't stop snapping the reigns until my legs became numb and stiff from riding in the hard saddle.

I pulled back on the reigns, roughly causing the horse to veer in retaliation. Once the beast settled down, I slid off the saddle, falling to my knees from the pain in my legs. I took in a deep breath, forcing myself to stand up on shaky limbs. Staggering to the horse, I untied the small sack of supplies meant for the stead's original owner before smacking him on the rear. The horse reared before galloping off back towards Fallbell. I waited for a second to see the horse plow through the woods before turning on my heels and walking in random zigzag motions making sure to step on places where a lot of leaves lay. Walking on dirt leaves tracks, right? A sigh left my lips as I kept walking.

When night took over, I was barely able to find a large tree with a decent sized hollow high up in it big enough for me to fit inside. Using the little bit of strength I have left, I got a proper grip on the rim of the hollow and pulled myself up and inside of it with shaky arms. Once I was able to roll myself inside, I stretched my legs out as far as the tiny space would allow me. Considering the area was limited, my knees still touched my chest even when I slouched lower to allow more room. An annoyed sigh was the only thing that could be heard as I tried to at least get comfortable.

While I sat in the tiny little space, thoughts of despair and sorrow plagued my consciousness. My brother- my dear Ricky, is dead. My mother is forever gone. My father… I'm the last one of my family alive. I am the last *one*! What am I supposed to do now? Do I look for the person who ordered the assassin to murder my family? Do I let it go and try to pursue a peaceful life? What about Hawk? Will he even give me a choice in the matter?

What am I supposed to do!

"Why is this happening...?" I whispered to myself, burying my face into my knees as the tears burst through. Thankfully, no dreams or nightmares came to me when I finally dozed off. There was only sweet darkness.

***

The unbearable ache that plagued my feet, the breathlessness and the pain that consumed my entire body made it extremely hard to continue walking. Actually, where am I going? Is there even another town on the other side of these woods? More importantly, is Hawk still following me? Just to be sure, I looked over my shoulder to see if he was there. When I saw nothing but trees, leaves, and a few woodland critters, my heart started to beat faster. Is he hiding? Is he close to me?

Where is he?

"... more!"

"Sir, as I said before, I will not have any more crate apples until tomorrow." Are those people arguing over produce? Using common sense, I can only deduce that there aren't two random strangers quarreling in the middle of the woods over a merchant's supply of apples.

I'm near a town!

A breath of adrenaline fueled my body to surge forward almost at a desperate pace to reach the people I could hear arguing.

"That's ridiculous! You said that two weeks ago! Why don't you ever have anything I ask for when I come by, huh?"

"That's because when you come, it's on the last day of the week! Everyone else has already bought all of my supplies!" I broke through the tree line and stumbled out onto the dirt road that the stall- or more like carriage- was set up. A few feet away was a bustling town with a few people here and there going about their business.

"Finally..." I whispered, stumbling forward before falling to my knees in utter exhaustion, the momentary adrenaline rush receding. As I lay panting on the ground, I felt more than saw a shadow cast over my body as one of the two men stood over me.

"Are you okay, ma'am?" The voice of the stall vendor echoed over me, concern and confusion etched into his words.

"Where did she come from?" the other man nearly shouted. "Is she one of them feral kids that live in the woods?" The vendor seemed to ignore the other man as he knelt beside me and lifted up my upper body from the ground, turning me around. After my eyes adjusted to the brightness of the sun behind him, I could make out his middle-aged face looking down at me in mild worry.

"Are you okay, ma'am? Do you need help?" I swallowed hard before pushing out of his grip and standing up on shaky legs. I staggered slightly, causing him to hold his arm out in case I fell, but I stood firm.

"I'm fine. I just… where am I?"

"Belhall."

"Belhall… I think I'll be fine. Thank you for your concern." I nodded in thanks before wandering off down the dirt road when a thought came to mind. Turning to look over my shoulder, I fixed the other man with a nasty glare. "Why don't you try and figure out if a person is okay before you accuse them of being insane." The man narrowed his eyes and stepped forward to say something else, but I turned my back to him and walked off.

As I made my way down the road of the little town, I noticed something that I've seen in the past three villages I've been to since coming to Rosesea- every single person is… *nice.* Every place I passed by, people went out of their way to ask if I was okay or if I needed anything. A kind man even gave me some bread to eat while I walked. This whole kindness thing is so surreal. Back in Clearapal, if there was a person in need lying on the street, most people would just keep walking, ignoring them. Only those of the lower-class would actually stop, but they wouldn't do anything in fear of wasting supplies they might need. Here in Rosesea, it's the complete opposite.

Are we really that shallow in Clearapal?

"What might the future hold for you? Would you like to see what could happen tomorrow? In five years? In ten years? Knowing all of these things can only cost you one little silver coin."

It can't be!

I looked around me almost frantically until my eyes landed on a lone stand set up in between two buildings. The stall was partially shrouded in darkness, concealing the woman who stood behind it, but that voice was unforgettable. I will never forget the woman who interrupted my philosophy class all those months ago and put that old grunt in his place. Walking swiftly towards the stall, I slammed my hands down on the table, getting close to the cloaked woman.

"Who are you?"

"I am who I am, and I'm not who I'm not." My eyes narrowed in annoyance as I reached out and snatched the hood from her head. Straight light brown hair fell down her back, landing just below her shoulders. Dark forest green eyes stared back at me as a smirk painted her lips.

"Let's not act cute right now." I nearly hissed leaning in closer. "What were you doing in my philosophy class in Clearapal nearly three months ago?" A mischievous glint glazed her eyes as she put a finger to her chin as if she were thinking the event over.

"I do vaguely remember speaking to an elderly man and a little girl who seemed obsessed with defying anything to do with authority, but what is it that you want me to tell you about that?"

"What were you doing there?"

"Why does it matter? It happened so long ago…" Her eyes drifted away from mine, staring off into the distance before they snapped back to me with a sly smirk on her face. "Do you believe that has something to do with what's happening now?"

"Just answer the question."

"You do realize that not everything has to do with you. Maybe I just wanted to attend a lesson and shared my opinion when I believed the teacher was wrong." I huffed, leaning back away from the stall standing up straight.

"I don't believe anything happens by chance anymore," I whispered, lowering my eyes to the stall covered in a black tarp. Everything was silent as the words echoed throughout my consciousness.

Everything is happening for a reason… but what reason is that?

"Dove." My head snapped up to her with a raised eyebrow.

"What?" A soft laugh left her lips.

"My name. It's Dove."

"Like the bird?"

"Yes, because I am a child born out of love." She used the back of her hands to frame her face creating an image of a heart. A smile spread across her face that seemed to shine with on otherworldly luster.

"Interesting… even though I didn't ask for it." She laughed softly before reaching out a hand towards me. Just as she was about to touch me, a loud yell was heard as all eyes turned towards a group of four guards standing six feet away from us.

"There's the con-artist! Get her!" The guards rushed forwards prepared to arrest Dove when she simply smiled and flipped the stall, causing the black tarp to momentarily block the guards' view. My heart pounded in my chest as adrenaline shot through my body.

Should I run?

"Go into the forest- it's the only place you'll be safe from the assassin," Dove whispered in my ear from behind me. My eyes widened as I swirled around, but she was already gone.

"After her!" The guards sprinted down the street, spreading out so they could check every street corner they could to find the elusive woman. I let out the breath I didn't know I was holding as I allowed myself to relax.

What just-

"It seems our game of cat and mouse has come to a close." My blood ran cold. Tears pricked at the corner of my eyes as the breath left my body. A sizeable gloved hand clasped onto my shoulder, holding me still with an iron grip. I don't have to look to know who the man- the *demon* that stood behind me is.

"How did you…" I started, but a chocked gasp cut off my words as a tear fell down my cheeks. His grip tightened as he leaned in closer to my ear only by the slightest of inches.

"If you scream, I'll have to kill everyone here." My heart seemed to stop beating as Hawk gently guided me away from the town and towards the vast jungle of a forest that no person has ever entered… and made it back out alive. As we broke through the forest line, the tears flooded my cheeks. Why is it so hard to breathe?

"You don't have to do this!" I shouted, knowing that, by now, we were too far away from the town for anyone to actually hear.

"I'm just following orders." He retorted with no emotion in his voice as he continued to force me to march onwards towards my death- to a cold, desolate place to kill me like he did my family.

I won't die today!

Using a strength I didn't know I had, I shoved my elbow backward. The grunt of pain and the feeling of his hand loosening on my shoulder brought a spark of hope through my system that made me turn around and punch him as hard as I could in his face. When his head jerked to the side, I twirled on my heels and took off.

I refuse to die here!

VIII

Branches reached out scratching at my skin, causing cuts and a few nasty bruises. Roots lifted above the ground tried their best to snag my feet to send me hurling down to the unforgiving forest floor to become an easy target to the more than angry assassin chasing after me. Considering this is the *second* time I've escaped his wrath, I doubt he will allow me a third. So, with adrenaline pumping through my veins and the terror of death lingering behind me, my legs kept moving forward.

I can get away- I can make it!

A short scream echoed through my lips as a knife buried itself into a tree I passed. A bullet almost hit my head as I started to run in a zigzag motion. A sharp pain raised from my right cheek as one of his knives nicked it before embedding itself into another tree.

Why won't he give up!

Out of the corner of my eye, a large oak tree that had a hollow cove in its base caught my attention. It looked big enough for me to fit but small enough to keep Hawk away. My limbs screamed as I bolted towards it, using all of my remaining strength. I could practically *feel* Hawk reaching his hand out- ready to grab me and drag me to my death.

I won't die here!

Hitting the ground, I used my momentum to slide the rest of the distance. A tidal wave of relief washed over me as the sight of bark consumed my vision, signaling that I was safely within the tree.

"I'm safe-" a scream etched through my lips as my body kept sliding downwards. My eyes widened as air surrounded me, a sensation of flying filled me. Amid my fear, I felt… free, but just as soon as the feeling came, it left me as the sight of the ground came into focus. My heart dropped as I threw my arms in front of me to break my fall. My body slammed into the ground, and my head smacked against a tree root before darkness took over.

***

Pounding in my skull woke me. The simple movement of trying to sit up caused the ache to increase tenfold. Deciding on staying still, I raised my hand to my head, but the feeling of warm liquid made me bring it to my blurry line of vision. The clear red blotch coating my fingers told me that I hit something with my head- hard.

Applying pressure to my head with my hand, I struggled to my feet. My legs shook terribly, and black spots dotted my vision. In the next moment, I was on my knees, staring blurrily at the ground below. Inhaling deeply, I, slowly, rose to my feet. This time, I was able to stay standing with minimal splotches in my vision.

"Where am I?" I took a step forward. The dots reappeared with a vengeance as nausea took hold.

Staggering forward, I found perch on a tree. Using it as support, I leaned my entire body against it, focusing on taking in deep breaths. When I trusted myself again to test standing on my own, I pushed away from the tree, keeping a cautious hand on the bark just in case. I stayed still until all the dots were gone before chancing a practice step forward. When I didn't fall, I let out a sigh of relief before once again, looking around me.

Everywhere I look are towering trees. Not the kind I've seen in the small woods surrounding the villages I've been too, but trees you only see in thick jungles that people never go into. Trees that grew thick branches and thousands upon thousands of leaves with vines interlocking some of them together while on the forest floor lay bushes and smaller trees that never had the chance to get to be such monstrous beings. Turning to look behind me, a short steep cliff about eight feet in the air sat on the edge beneath a large oak tree, a rather large hole leading to me at its base.

"How did I get here?" I mumbled to myself, looking around me for any signs of where I was headed. Almost like a smack in the face, images of Hawk, Dove, a knife, my father, my mother- *Ricky!*

A tear slid down my cheek, stinging the open wounds it crossed. The weight of the grief I felt sent me staggering backward against a tree. Taking in a sharp breath, I fought back the tears closing my eyes slowly. I've cried enough- I've allowed myself to be the victim for too long! I *will* find out who did this, and I *will* get justice for my family one way or another.

Just replace the sadness with rage.

I coached myself. The feeling of my tears drying up brought a small smirk to my lips.

"I will have justice," I whispered to myself, pushing away from the tree, standing up tall. "I won't let anyone get in my way." The sound of rustling in the bushes not too far from me set my entire being on edge.

Is it Hawk? Has he found me?

I won't let him take me down without a fight!

I shouted in my mind. Turning around towards the tree, I searched for the lowest branch thin enough for me to break but thick enough to do some damage. When I found one, I reached up, and, using all of my body weight, I snapped the branch off. Holding it out in front of me like a bat, I readied for that cursed assassin to show his face.

The longer the seconds ticked by, the tenser I became in anticipation.

Just come out already!

Then, a shadowed silhouette emerged from the brush. I raised my branch, ready to swing. Dark red fur and beady brown eyes staring back at me from three feet off of the ground sent a wave of disappointment settling through my veins. A fox?

As if he had no idea of the mental anguish he just put me through, the little fox sat down and began to lick its paw in pure contentment. A sigh left my lips as I took a step towards the little animal prepared to shoo it away. A loud raspy yell that almost sounded childish echoed before a pudgy ball of flesh flew from the brush attacking the defenseless fox. The sound of the fox screeching in pain sent a sick feeling through my body. I scrambled away from the from the small child-like beast as it killed the fox and began doing something to its corpse that I refused to watch.

The beast stopped in its tracks and raised its oversized head to the sky sniffing. It froze for a second before twirling around towards me. The sight of blood covering its large mouth filled with tiny sharpened teeth and the black beads that made up its eyes staring back at me made my jaw drop.

What is that thing!

It let out a disgusting laugh as it bounded towards me, its mouth opened wide.

I said I'm not dying today!

Getting a tight grip on the branch, I swung, knocking it out of the air. I didn't wait to watch it hit the ground as I scrambled to my feet and began running away. The sound of quick tiny feet- almost like a child's- running behind me sent my mind on edge.

What-!

"Ah!" My legs, trapped in the beast's pudgy arms, stopped moving, sending me slamming into the ground.

The feeling of the fiend's tiny hands climbing up my body towards my head sent a chill of terror down my spine. Swinging out with my fists and kicking the air with my legs, I tried to get the thing off of me, but the sight of its rotting teeth and lifeless black depths glaring back at me as it made an unnatural laugh sent a paralyzing fear through me. A tear slid down my cheeks as it raised its little fist wielding a dirty, bloodied knife ready to kill me.

No!

A vein wrapped itself around its torso, yanking it off me. Panting frantically, I quickly moved into a sitting position, scrambling away until my back hit a tree. I watched in awe as the beast was dragged towards someone covered in a cloak. The little beast tried it's hardest to escape by trying to get a grip in the dirt using its tiny fingers. The cloaked figure pulling it towards them didn't even seem to struggle with dragging the thing despite its efforts.

When the thing was close, the hooded figure bent down and picked it up by the loose skin on the back of its neck as if it were a cat. With a flick of their wrist, the child-like fiend was sent hurtling through the air before smashing into a tree. Its body slid down, crashing to the ground. From the way its chest slowly raised and fell, I could tell it wasn't dead, but why didn't the person kill it? It's a monster!

"What's a human doing out here?" My eyes snapped back to the man who saved me as he knocked his hood back. The first thing that came to my attention was his ears. They weren't… *natural.* They were long and pointed with small red rubies pierced at the tips. "Oh my- are you one of those deaf or mute humans?" I blinked in shock as he took a step closer to me.

"I… what… I…"

"Goodness- you can't even speak properly!" He complained, striding straight towards me. My eyes widened further as I scrambled back. When my hand bumped the branch I dropped, I snatched it holding it in front of me as a shield.

"Stay back!" He didn't even stop as he smacked the branch out of my hands and took hold of my wrist.

I'm not going to die here!

Punching, kicking, clawing- I did anything to get him to let go, but he just seemed annoyed with my efforts as he began to drag me in a direction.

"Let me go!" I screeched, dropping my body to the ground forcing him to drag me.

He sighed, letting go. I crawled away from him, my breath more labored then it's ever been. He knelt in front of me, glaring intensely into my eyes. That's when I noticed- his eyes are purple! Not just any kind of purple, but a rich dark purple that almost looked like dusty jewels.

"I see the problem," He suddenly said, reaching out and flicking my head where my gash was. I let out a pained cry as I smacked his hand away gingerly, holding my now aching head. "You're suffering from a head injury. There's hope for you yet." He stood back up and walked over to the beast. He untied his vein from around it's body and rolled it back up before storing it within one of the sacks attached to his leather belt.

"What- what are you?" I shouted. He didn't even pause in his work as he began to straighten out his belt.

"A male, or do you not know the difference between male and female?" I glared at his back.

"You know what I meant, you jerk! What are you? I've never seen a human with features like yours." He finally turned around and glanced at me.

"And?"

"And?"

"Yes, and?"

"What are you talking about?"

"What?"

"Stop it!" I shouted as a smirk played on his lips. "If you won't tell me that much, can you at least give me your name?"

"No."

"Why not?"

"I don't know you, lady. You might be some psycho."

Deep breathes, stay calm.

"Look, you seem strong, and I need someone strong to help me. You see, there's this crazy-"

"I don't see how this is my problem, lady."

"I was just getting to that-"

"Not my problem." And with that, he turned his back to me and began to walk away. My jaw dropped as I ran up behind him, stopping a few feet away from him.

"So that's it? You're not even going to hear me out?"

"I don't see how I will benefit from doing so." He called over his shoulder, still walking away. Panic set inside of me as I swallowed hard running after him.

"Fine, then go! Be a coward who leaves someone who's in distress!"

"You're not in distress. You're an annoyance looking to give me a headache."

"You're a jerk!" He paused and turned around, giving me a leveled look.

"And you're an idiot. Haven't your parents ever told you not to talk to strangers?"

"They have, but right now, strangers are all I have."

"That sounds like a personal problem you should keep to yourself."

"Don't you have any compassion?"

"I do, but not for strays."

"Then, do you have compassion for someone who's lost their entire family?" He stared at me for a while before turning himself entirely towards me.

"Why are you dumping your personal issues on me? You don't even know my name."

"I asked!" I hollered in disbelief.

"I'm sensing some major hostility from you, and I don't appreciate it," I swear if he wasn't the only person in this forsaken jungle I would have left by now.

Deep breathes...deep breathes.

"Alright, then, what is your name?"

"I don't feel comfortable speaking to someone I don't know."

"Okay, that's understandable." I gritted from between my teeth as I forced a smile to my face.

Deep breathes... stay calm.

"My name is Jayde Henryk, and you are?" Extending out my hand towards him in a show- or more like faked- kindness. He stared at my hand for a minute before moving his eyes back up to meet mine.

"I don't want to tell you."

"What?"

"You're so foolish."

"What are you talking about?" I half screamed in frustration.

"Don't you know better than to take what a fairy says seriously?" My jaw dropped as realization filled me.

"Great, now I understand- he's crazy." I turned my back on him and began to walk away.

"I wouldn't go that way if I were you." He called from behind me.

"Oh yeah, like I'm going to take the advice of a delusional jerk!" I shouted back, continuing on in the opposite direction of him.

Maybe there's water nearby?

Almost on impulse, I turned around to see if that crazy man was still standing there so I could ask him, but I had already made it out of his sight. I sighed and turned back around. Out of nowhere, my feet snagged against an invisible force and sent me slamming to the ground. A groan of pain escaped my lips as I craned my neck to see what I tripped over.

A wire?

"Yeaaaah!" A familiar raspy voice screeched. My eyes widened as another of those hideous child-like monsters came running towards me, holding a wooden ax in its hands.

"What-!" Fear consumed me as I crawled away from it. The closer it came, the more my lungs burned..

Stay calm! Breathe!

Right, when it was in range, I lifted my foot to kick it, but a dark figure dropped from the sky behind the little beast startling both of us.

"There you are." The crazy man said as he snatched up the creature by the loose skin on the back of its neck, just like the last one. The beast shook with fear as it was turned around to stare into deep purple eyes. "Hold still." His taunting tone scared the little thing so bad that it seemed to… die? Well, it stopped moving. A smirk formed on his lips as he picked off a few of the scarce strands of hairs on the top of the beast's head before dropping it to the ground. He opened one of the pouches on his right hip and pulled out a small clear vial. Placing the hairs into it, he stored the bottle back into the bag before turning his back to me and beginning to walk away. "Thanks for the help, foolish girl!"

"You knew that would happen?" A gasp escaped my lips. I pushed myself from the ground and chased after him, red lining my vision. "You used me as bait!"

"I told you not to come this way."

"But, you didn't tell me that another of those things was hiding on the path!"

"For one, those things have names. They are called hobbes. Two, I am not obligated to tell you these things because I'm not responsible for you. Now, leave me alone." As he walked passed me, I found myself frozen in place. Hobbes? Fairies? Those are fictional- nothing more than fairytales!

Then how do you explain the thing that attacked twice?

My eyes slowly drifted over to the still unconscious hobbe lying on the ground, its abnormal large mouth open with a purple tongue hanging out. Its foot twitched, sending a jolt of fear through me.

"Wait!" I shouted, whirling around on my heel and racing towards the mysterious stranger.

A mysterious stranger that has saved my life twice now.

"Stop following me, you weird woman!" He shouted over his shoulder.

"Why did you use me as bait? Why did you take that Hobbe's hair?"

"Ma'am, my mother taught me not to tell my business to strangers. Haven't you ever heard the story of the curious cat?"

"I think I have a right to know when my life was put in danger to get it!"

"If you must know, I was hunting for a hobbe with hair because I'm doing something that requires them. As you have seen, these little guys aren't the bravest on Earth, and they know fairies are stronger than they are. So, to catch one, I needed bait. Just as luck would have it, a foolish human decided to jump off a cliff and land near a hobbe den. That stupid human is you, by the way." He added with a mocking smirk on his face. I licked my lips slowly in a way that forced me to think about my next set of words before I said them.

"I figured that much." I ground out, crossing my arms under my chest. "And I must say I don't appreciate being called stupid because I didn't *decide* to fall down a hill because I didn't *know* it was a hill."

"But you did slide down one for no reason so, therefore, you are still a foolish idiot."

"I was being chased, you moron!"

"And where exactly is this invisible pursuer of yours? Oh, is he hiding behind a tree waiting to attack?" I pursed my lips together as I lowered my eyes, looking around. Is he really waiting in the trees? Is he waiting for this stranger to leave before he kills me?

"Whatever, I don't have to make you believe me, but the fact that my life is in danger is real. I don't care if you're some fairy or hobbe or whatever- you seem to be strong, and I need all the help I can get. So, if you can find it in your heart to help me, then I will do whatever I can to repay you, but if you decide to leave me out here to die a miserable death… I will respect your decision." He gave me a leveled look for a long time before his eyes narrowed slightly.

"Are you trying to guilt-trip me into helping you?"

"I'm just telling you the truth." There was a long pause before he spoke again.

"I'll consider helping you if you tell me why this person is after you."

"That's what I'm trying to figure out."

"Alright then, when you figure it out, then I'll help you." My jaw dropped as he began to walk away.

"That's the whole reason I need your help!" I screamed, whirling around towards him.

"Then you shouldn't have asked!" He shouted back.

That's it!

"You're a complete jerk!" I screamed, picking up a rock and chucking it at him. He easily dodged, moving his head to the right. Turning around, a mocking smirk on his face, he stuck his tongue out.

"Sucks to be you, doesn't it?" Anger bubbled in my chest as I opened my mouth to show him how it feels to be ridiculed when a dangerous glare covered his face. Anger momentarily forgotten, I raised a brow in confusion. Before I could ask him what was going on, he snapped his head up as two blobs fell from the trees landing right on top of him, knocking him to the ground.

"We found you big brother!" the two blobs giggled as they sat up on top of him. Said brother groaned as he shoved them off him.

"Claribel, Eallair, what are you two doing here? I told both of you not to follow me." The two identical-looking children- one a little girl and the other a little boy- sat on their butts where they had been shoved, holding their heads down in shame.

"But brother, we just wanted to see what you were doing so we can become awesome like you!" Claribel, the girl, shouted back. Though her words sounded sincere, there was a calculating shine within their depths as if she knew what she was saying would get her out of trouble with her brother. Unfortunately for the twins, their *adoring* big brother seemed to see straight through her ploy.

"You two should know by now that my ego is far too big for subtle flattery, such as that to influence my decisions." He glared hard down at the two of them before pointing in the direction he was heading. "Now, get going. Mother is going to kill me if she finds out you two wondered off looking for me."

"Yes, big bro-"

"Who is she, Singer?" Eallair asked, turning his entire body towards me. His light purple eyes that shined with mischievous ideas were hazed over with wonder.

"That's a stalker, now get away from it and let's go." Singer, the jerk I've been speaking to for the past hour it seems, said motioning impatiently for the two children to follow him. Ignoring him, I turned my full attention down to the little boy with a welcoming smile on my face.

"My name is Jayde. What's yours?" Bright pink dusted his cheeks as he averted his eyes to the ground kicking a leaf with his foot.

"Eallair…" he mumbled, twisting his body in a nervous show. My smile widened as I flicked his nose lightly, eliciting a soft giggle from him.

"That's a wonderful name, much better than Singer." I teased shooting a victorious smirk towards the older male as the younger two laughed.

"My name is Claribel! Is my name wonderful too?" The little girl gushed bounding to my side with hope sparkling in her dark pink eyes. I pat the top of her head as I nodded.

"Of course!" She yelped in victory as she jumped up and down in excitement. The loud huff from Singer brought a wicked smirk to my face. "What's wrong *Singer*, are you jealous?"

"Not in the slightest, you headache."

"You're just jealous your name isn't as cool as ours."

"The day I'm jealous of you will be the day I throw myself off of a cliff into a pit of carnivorous sea monsters." I narrowed my eyes, the undying need to best him in this simple verbal match taking over me.

"Do they call you Singer because you like to sing?"

"They don't call you Jayde because you're a jewel." A silent battle to the death raged as neither Singer nor I spoke. Our eyes did all the talking.

"Well, I think you're beautiful!" Eallair shouted, taking hold of my hand. I felt Claribel take the other, but I never took my eyes off Singer.

"I think mother will love her too!"

"Yeah, let's take her to mother!" before I could even register what was happening, I was being dragged behind the two laughing children as Singer trailed behind us yelling at them to leave me be.

What have I gotten myself into?

IX

"Come on, Jayde!"

"Yeah, hurry up, Jayde!" The twins giggled as they continued to drag me behind them in their race to wherever we were going.

"Where are you taking me?"

"To our mother!" Claribel laughed as she pushed tree branches from her path, jumped over roots, and sidestepped tree stumps.

In the next second, we burst through the full array of trees into a small clearing with a single cottage sitting on the edge. It resembles the one I had in Redmage- small and comfortable. Granted, there were vines and other forms of greenery growing all around the expanse of it. Patches of beautiful flowers that I've never seen before covered the ground around it, almost like a wild garden.

"Do you like our home?" Claribel asked, tugging my arm in her excitement.

"You can't force her to like it, Claribel!" Eallair reprimanded before turning his soft kind eyes up to me. "Mother takes care of the garden- that's why it looks so pretty."

"It's gorgeous," I responded to both of them, lifting my head back to the house. It truly is beautiful. Just then, the front door opened, and a gorgeous woman walked out.

Her long, nearly red, brown hair flowed behind her as she closed the door, holding a woven basket in her hands. Her pointed ears poking out of her hair twitched slightly before she turned her attention towards us. Her pink eyes narrowed in anger as she placed a hand on her hip.

"Now, where have the two of you been? I've been worried sick about you!" Both Claribel and Eallair lowered their heads in trepidation before Claribel whined in protest.

"But mother- we just wanted to play with Singer! Plus, we found a new playmate." The little girl pulled me forward with a smile shining on her face. "Her name is Jayde, and she said that we have beautiful names!" I blinked at the woman.

Am I supposed to bow or something?

"Uh, hello ma'am-"

"You're just adorable!" She squealed, dropping the basket in her rush. My eyes widened as the woman wrapped her arms around my neck in a bone-crushing embrace.

"Mother, don't hog Jayde- she's our playmate!" Eallair pouted, crossing his arms over his chest.

"Oh, hush!" The woman turned her gaze back to me, a sparkle shining deep within those pink depths. "Your name is Jayde, right?"

"Yes."

"That is such a precious name! Where did you come from?" Her hand grazed over my head, hovering just above where a consistent dull ache started. "How did you get hurt?"

"I-"

"Mother, stop encouraging it- it won't leave if you give it attention," Singer called from his perch up in a tree above us. He gazed down at us, lazily with a glint of annoyance coating his purple eyes.

A frown marred the woman's lips as she held her palm facing upwards. Out of thin air, a rock materialized in her hand to which she chucked at Singer. The stone hit the proud male right in his forehead, making him plummet from his branch down to the ground, landing in a bush.

Is he okay?

He groaned in pain as he sat up, rubbing the sore spot on his head.

Yeah, he's fine.

"I will not tolerate any more of your rude behavior to this wonderful human girl." The woman scolded before she turned a pleasant smile towards me. "Besides, I want to keep her! She's just so adorable!" The woman gushed.

"I can't-"

"Come inside and rest yourself!" She hooked her arm with mine in an iron grip and basically forced me to walk with her into the little cottage.

I tried to free my arm, or at least loosen her grip on me, but the stubborn woman wouldn't budge.

At least now I see where that egotistical jerk gets his social skills from.

Sighing, I resigned myself to my fate and went along with the woman's demands.

As the door opened, revealing the inside of the cottage, my jaw hit the floor. The cabin wasn't a small one-story home as I thought it was. In fact, it's two stories- the second floor being the one we entered from, and the first floor is below us. From where we started, there was a grand living room spacious enough to host a party of about twelve people and still have ample space for dancing.

There weren't any couches or fireplaces. Instead, hammocks were hanging from high suspended tree limbs that stuck out from the corners of the room. In the back was an open banister that overlooked the ground floor. The bottom floor was what a typical cottage would look like. A kitchen furnished with a dining table and stove. A living room with chairs that resembled bushes instead of couches, a large fireplace, and windows that overlooked a beautiful meadow, and much more that was out of sight.

"Come Jayde, let's go downstairs so we can talk."

"But ma'am I-"

"Oh, please, call me Lilly!" She gushed, guiding me to the back of the room and down a set of spiral stairs.

"Alright then, Lilly, I can't stay."

"Nonsense! Of course, you can!"

"No, I really can't. If I do, then I would be putting you and your family in danger." Lilly glanced at me from the corner of her eye before she waved me off.

"Darling, no human chasing you can harm my family or you while you're here."

"Which won't be for long," Singer called from his place at the head of the dining table.

"How did you-"

"See mother? She doesn't know anything about us. She can't even form a coherent sen-" Lilly materialized next to him, smacking him. Singer let out a grunt of pain as he rubbed his head. Lilly towered over him with a glare that promised painful repercussions.

"I will not tell you again, Singer. Be nice to Jayde. If you cost me a chance of having a cute human around, then I'll punish you in the most creative way I can think of." Singer huffed but didn't say anything.

This woman is terrifying.

Sweat dampened my forehead as a nervous smile formed on my lips.

"Its fine Lilly, he's not saying anything worth listening to anyway." Lilly turned a frown towards me before focusing her attention back to Singer.

"Go and pour a few glasses of my special tea for our guest."

"They say you shouldn't feed stray animals, or else they won't leave." A loud smack echoed through the cottage.

"Now!" A smirk broke out on Singer's lips as he obediently stood and disappeared into the kitchen to do as his mother asked. "I swear that boy is going to be alone forever with an attitude like his." A sigh broke through her lips as she sat down at the table, putting her face in her palm.

"Maybe if you change his personality, then someone will think he's decent," I mumbled, sitting down at the table next to her. Her ear twitched as she turned her pink eyes towards me.

"You don't think he's a decent boy?"

"What?"

"Now that I think about it, you don't really seem bothered by how my son acts." A twinkle entered her eyes as she seemed to light up with excitement. "Would you be interested in my son?"

"What? Wait, what are you-?"

"He is a good boy, I promise! He may be rough around the edges with that mouth of his-" a loud dramatic gasp left her lips as her hands flew to her face. "Since you both are so adorable, you would make the cutest grandchildren!" My jaw hit the floor as I backed away from the crazy woman in complete shock.

Grand-what?

"Uh, I just met your son, and I don't think-"

"Nonsense! You'll grow to love him!"

"Ma'am I-"

"I told you to call me Lilly- no wait, call me mom!" She giggled like an elated schoolgirl as she clasped her hands together and let out a dreamy sigh.

"I still say we shouldn't feed the stray. She might come back later wanting more free stuff." Singer announced as he walked back in the room, holding a tray with four cups filled with a green liquid.

"Singer, do I need to have a conversation with you about being kind to your future wife?"

"My future what?"

"Is it true that you're a family of fairies?" I quickly interjected, hoping they couldn't see the red tinge on my cheeks. Seriously, what is wrong with this woman?

"Of course, we are dear." Lilly laughed, handing me a cup of tea. Not really thinking much of it, I took a large sip of it, noting the sweetness and creamy texture.

"But fairies aren't real." She stared at me for a long while before letting out a bellowing howl.

"Are you from Clearapal?"

"Yes, why do you ask?"

"Darling, everyone knows that humans in Clearapal don't believe in our existence because there are so few of us still living there."

"And why is that?"

"Because of the lack of an adequate forest and a large number of hostile humans, not many of any creature would like to call it home."

"But what about the humans in Rosesea? Aren't some of them hostile too?"

"Darling, the keyword in that sentence is *some*. Our numbers in Rosesea are too great for such a small group to pose a threat. Besides, most humans in Rosesea are friendly towards most faye." I raised a brow as she took a long sip of her tea.

"What are faye?"

"Magical creatures, darling. There are many- fairies, Hobbes, goblins, and ogres, just to name a few."

"Then you really are fairies?" She set her teacup on the table, a small smile on her face.

"Yes!" she laughed, "Has my son told you nothing?"

"Well, he did, but I also believed he was insane at the time. It's more believable coming from someone more levelheaded like you." A soft laugh left her lips.

"You wouldn't be the first to say that." She mused, running her finger along the rim of her cup. "Like I said before, we are a family of fairies."

"But, none of you have… you know wings and stuff." Her bellowing laugh filled the air.

"What stories have you humans been coming up with?" I opened my mouth to say something, but the sound of the door beside the fireplace opening cut me off.

A tall male with dark purple eyes and a muscular build walked in with the same elongated ears with obsidian earrings pierced at the tips. His eyes connected with mine before they turned to Lilly.

"Lilly, why is there a human in our home?"

"Claribel and Eallair brought the stray here," Singer called from the archway of the kitchen. Lilly snapped her head to him with a sickly-sweet smile plastered on her face.

"Singer, please follow me to the kitchen to get… more tea." Singer opened his mouth, but Lilly was out of her chair and dragging him into the kitchen before he could even get a word out of his mouth.

Shortly after, the sounds of multiple smacks and a soft groan of pain leaked into the room before Lilly emerged a few minutes later, a bright, happy smile on her face. The man gave her a suspicious look before walking cautiously to the table.

"Lilly?"

"In a moment dear." Lilly then turned her full attention to me. "I apologize for my son's deplorable behavior, darling. I can assure you he is very sorry."

"I'd believe that more if I heard it from his mouth," I mumbled. Lilly raised a brow sitting back down.

"What do you mean?"

"I mean that he knows what I'm doing here, and he still insists on saying all of these horrible things to me!" I finally snapped, shooting to my feet.

Honestly, where does that guy get off? Who calls someone who has just lost their home, their family- everything that means anything to them a homeless stray? Who insists on casting out someone who needs urgent help as if their suffering was a nuisance?

"What are you talking about?"

My heart skipped a beat. Did I really just say that?

"I-"

"The stray told me something that she should have kept to herself." Singer grumbled from the kitchen. Lilly shot a warning glare in his direction.

"Lilly, what is going on?" the man asked confusedly.

"Hush for a moment, Anar." Lilly, again, turned her attention back to me, her eyes softened. "Tell me what happened, darling." Tears weld up in my eyes as I gasped.

"Everyone… everyone is gone. My mother… my father… my *brother*! Everyone- they were all murdered! Now someone is trying to murder me, and I don't know why!" Lilly's eyes widened.

"Wha-"

"Everywhere I go, he's there! He's always waiting for me! I can't sleep without worrying about him killing me! Its torture!" warm arms latched around my body, rocking me gently while I cried.

"Hush now darling, hush. You're safe here." She whispered in my ear, smoothing my hair down that I have no doubt was stuck up from my misadventures in the forests.

"What I fail to see is when this became our problem?" Lilly sent a nasty glare to Singer as he slowly hobbled from the kitchen to the table, nursing his bruised head in his hands.

"Singer, do we need to have another conversation about being kind to your future wife?"

"Mother, we don't need to have another chat about that, nor will she ever become my wife." He responded before turning his attention back to me. "I just want to know why she calls me heartless about something that has nothing to do with me." Anger boiled inside of me as I pushed away from Lilly, glaring hatefully at the heartless man. I opened my mouth to yell- to *scream* at him when the other male in the room cleared his throat rather loudly.

"I think it is high time someone told me what is going on."

"Oh, yes, I almost forgot!" Lilly shouted, a smile spreading across her lips. "This is Jayde, Singer's future wife. Singer and the twins found Jayde on the edge of the forest, running away from an assassin. A hobbe tried to attack her, and that is when her future husband swooped in and saved her!" Lilly exclaimed, clapping her hands together.

"I'm pretty sure it didn't happen like that." Singer deadpanned, giving her a strange look.

"Then," Lilly said a little louder than needed, completely disregarding Singer. "They brought her here to meet me. Oh!" She turned her happy smile to me, gesturing towards the man. "This is my husband, and you're soon to be father-in-law, Anar." I nodded absently as I gave the new man a once over before turning my attention back to Lilly.

"I think it's sweet and flattering that you want me to be your daughter, but I can't- not now at least. I can't have peace while my family's murder goes unsolved- especially with the murderer still loose. I have to find out why this happened." A soft frown settled on her lips.

"Well, we can't have that, now, can we?" She mused to herself, moving to the table and sitting down. "Maybe, if we help you find the answers you're looking for, then you will marry my son?"

"That's not-"

"I got it!" She nearly yelled, snapping her fingers. "How about Singer goes with you to find the answers? That way, you both can bond and learn more about each other!"

"What?"

"Mother."

"Yes, dear?" Lilly asked in a sickly sweet voice.

"Let's say I entertain the idea after weighing the options of facing your tortures or the torment of being in that stray's company, how will I be able to help her?"

"Oh, that's simple! Just take her to the fairy queen."

"Fairy queen?" Lilly turned her attention to me, nodding.

"Yes, the fairy queen. She sees and knows everything. If anyone has answers to your questions, it would be her."

"That's fantastic and all that, but neither I nor anyone else for that matter knows where she is." Lilly snapped her head in Singer's direction, a dark aura surrounding her.

"Then, I suggest you figure out another way to help her, or do you want to take your chances with what my imagination can come up with to punish you?" Singer stared at his mother for a moment before his eyes drifted over to Anar.

"Listen to your mother." The older man simply said, settling himself at the table before taking the last teacup from the tray. Singer let out an annoyed sigh.

"Alright, fine, I'll take the stray to the fairy queen."

"Good, do you have any idea of how to find her?" Singer averted his eyes to the side.

"I might know someone who can help us."

Lilly wasted no time kicking us out once the plans were made. After throwing each of us a medium-sized satchel with a few supplies inside, she ordered us to either come back ready to be married or not at all.

"I want you two to look out for each other, which means you better not let anything happen to this adorable human, Singer!" Honestly, does anyone here know how to greet strangers?

"Well, it looks like I'm stuck with you until you solve your personal problems- which I'm almost positive won't happen- or you die which, I'm not going to lie, is way more likely." Apparently not.

"Look, I don't know what hit you on the head as a baby, but common sense says that you should be nice to strangers or at least sympathetic to those who have been through something traumatic."

"Common sense says not to speak to strangers, yet here you are."

"I wouldn't need to speak to strangers if I actually knew people that are crazy enough to live in a nightmarish forest like this."

"I'm going to let you decide how much sense that made." Singer turned his back to me and began walking away, probably hoping I wouldn't follow him.

That evil... lunatic!

"For your information that made perfect sense!"

"Whatever you say, foolish little stray."

"Stop calling me that!" He grunted, glancing around like he's searching for something. I narrowed my eyes at the back of his head.

First, he's tormenting me, then he's mocking my intelligence, and now he's outright ignoring me?

Suddenly, he stopped walking, almost causing my nose to smack into his back. Whirling around, he held a finger to his lips.

"Stay here and shut up, stray." My eyes narrowed until I was glaring spitefully at him.

"Why? Are you trying to abandon me?"

"I don't have to help you, you know. I can take a scolding from my mother better than I can take stupidity from a stray." I opened my mouth to yell at him- scream at the top of my lungs how much I despised him, but nothing came out.

Hasn't someone else threatened to leave me on my own to die before?

An image of my father's crazed face while he laughed manically entered my thoughts.

If he wants to leave, then let him!

Without saying anything else to the insufferable jerk, I brushed passed him walking in a different direction than he's going.

What do I need him for? I can figure this out on my own!

Taking in a deep, shaky breath to expel any semblance of fear left in me, I stood up straighter and marched on. As if being hit by a sack of bricks, my feet stopped.

Am I just doing what he wants? He doesn't deserve such a light punishment! If I'm such a nuisance, then I'll make him suffer by staying with him!

"Right after I give him a sound verbal thrashing for all the trouble he's put me through," I growled to myself. With my resolve in check and a new wind of direction, I whirled around on my heels and began the short trek back.

After I'm through with him, he'll think twice before he says something nasty to me-

"Ta ra ja!" a demonic voice roared. A green beast that towered slightly over me stood in my path, wielding a club in its hands. Killing intent surrounded it nearly suffocating me in its wrath. A scream ripped through my throat as it lunged at me, swinging its club in a vertical motion to lop off my head with the sheer force of the blow. Dropping to the ground, I kicked out as hard as I could, knocking the creature out of the sky. It landed with a loud bang on the ground just a few feet away from me.

"Why is it that you always choose to make yourself easy prey?" Singer sighed, dropping down from the trees behind it. When it saw him with its massive reptilian eyes, it tried to lunge, but Singer dodged easily before hitting it hard on the back of its neck. With one final grunt, it landed in a heap on the ground.

"What is that thing?" I can clearly tell it's not a hobbe. For one, it's taller- the hobbe was barely at knee level. This thing has shorter ears, a long pointy nose with a few warts dotted around it, and a thin body- it's hideous!

"Okay, I'm starting to feel offended since you keep calling everything you see a 'thing'."

"Then what is it?" I almost yelled, pushing off the ground to stand on my feet.

"Well, aren't we snippy?" A smirk formed on his lips before he turned his attention to the beast lying on the ground. Pulling out the dagger strapped to his belt, He cut off some of its toenails and placed them into a vial similar to the one he put the Hobbe's hairs in.

"What are you doing with that?"

"Nosey, aren't we?" He stood up straight, placing the vial into a pouch before brushing past me. "Unless you want to be out here when night falls, I suggest you hurry up and follow me." Turning on my heels, I watched his retreating back incredulously.

Is he seriously ignoring me again?

"Come on, stray! I want to spend as little time as possible with you!"

Please let me solve this mystery before I end up killing this insufferable man!

***

By mid-day- five hours from when we started- we walked at least fifteen miles. I know this because my legs were screaming bloody murder at me while I did the same to Singer. I swear- the man is a slave driver! He only allowed two breaks within the period that we walked in that only lasted for about five minutes before we were walking again. Honestly, how can anyone stand to travel like this?

"Singer, can we *please* stop? My legs are *killing me*!" Without waiting for a response, I halted plopping ungracefully onto a small boulder rubbing my feet gingerly. How many blisters do I have on my feet now? Seventy?

"I thought you said you weren't going to let anything get in your way from finding out the truth." He mocked, coming to a standstill in front of me, his arms crossed over his chest.

"And nothing will, but what good will it do me if I don't have feet to walk on?" I shot back without looking at him, my full attention on my foot massage.

Nothing can compare to how heavenly this feels!

"You know, if you continue to hold me back like this, I'm going to leave you here to fend off ogres by yourself."

"Ogres?" My head snapped up to meet his mocking purple eyes. A smirk played on his lips as he nodded, standing up straighter.

"Yes, ogres. Since they have such a severe allergy to the sun, they only come out during the night. They're vicious monsters that everyone avoids. In their eyes, everything with a pulse is food- including you." The smirk on his face only grew at my widened eyes.

"Then where can we stay to get away from them?"

"That's where we're headed if you would stop being such a weak little stray and hurry up." Wrapping his fingers around my wrist, he yanked me from the rock and half dragged me behind him.

"Will you let me go- don't drag me!"

"Then walk, you annoying stray!"

"I am not a stray!"

"Hush stray, you'll scare the animals away."

"What-"

Before I could finish, Singer already had his hand over my mouth, an expression that clearly said I should be quiet covering his face. Releasing my wrist, he turned around and continued walking through a denser section of trees. Swatting away an occasional low hanging branch, Singer finally stilled in his movements before looking over his shoulder at me.

"Good news, your loudmouth didn't scare them off."

"Shut up." I moved beside him using more force than needed to push the branch, blocking my view to whatever Singer's talking about.

Apparently, the dense forest was because this area was vacant of trees making up a large clearing. Roaming around and grazing within it was a large herd of horses. What surprised me was the fact that these were ordinary, four-legged horses.

"What- no Pegasus or unicorns?"

"What are you talking about? Those don't exist, weirdo." My jaw dropped as Singer strolled casually into the clearing without a care in the world.

Did he honestly just say that?

I took in a calming breath before following him. Besides, He can't defend me from Hawk if I kill him, right?

All of the horses paused in their grazing to watch us.

Are they going to attack?

I'm convinced that Singer basically read my mind as he glanced over his shoulder. His eyes practically became a second sun with the amount of pure amusement dancing within them before he turned his attention forward. Finally, he stopped by two horses- one pure black and the other a chestnut brown. Petting the black one, a soft smile formed on Singer's lips while he tenderly smoothed out the beast's mane.

"How have you been, boy?" The horse nudged his broad snout into Singer's face making a sound of approval that caused the smile to spread on Singer's face. Turning his attention to the other horse, Singer repeated the same greeting. "And how have you been, girl? Getting into more fights with Shadow?" The horse veered its head in a nodding motion before nuzzling the side of Singer's face.

Singer grunted in a sound similar to laughter, continuing to pet both horses. While watching, a warm feeling spread through my chest that I can't name.

So he does have a heart- no matter how small it may be.

As if feeling my eyes on him, Singer slowly dropped his hands to his side and turned towards me with a mocking smirk on his face.

"Have you ever ridden bareback before, stray?"

"I refuse to acknowledge anything you say when you call me that." I snapped.

"And I can refuse to help you and tell my mother you accidentally killed yourself in a tragic accident due to your own stupidity. With your mental capacity, it wouldn't be too hard to believe." I glared at him, taking a small step forward, wary of the two horses at Singer's side.

"For your information, I *have* ridden bareback before." He grunted before pointing to the black stallion with a small smirk on his face.

"This is Shadow, and this," He pointed to the other steed, "is Noel. They both are wild horses that I've been riding since they were ponies. Now, taking into account that you would probably die trying to ride Shadow, you may ride Noel. Since she's just as feisty as you, you'll make great friends." I glared at him before moving towards the chestnut stallion, its big brown eyes following my every move. I held my hands up in a non-threatening gesture.

"Good girl," I cooed, slowly putting a hand on its mane before gently smoothing out the hair. "I'm friendly, see?"

"To who?" I shot a nasty glare to Singer before turning my full attention to the horse. When she seemed alright with my presence, I moved to her side. After a couple of tries, I was able to hoist myself onto Noel's back. Once I steadied myself, I turned a triumphant smirk to Singer, who merely returned it.

"Good, you're competent enough to get on a horse. Now, stay on." He quickly mounted the bigger stallion. Placing a firm kick to its sides, the horse lurched forward into a sprint. On instinct, Noel lunged forward to follow, almost throwing me off of her back in the process. So, as I held on to her mane for dear life, I could only glare in half fear and half malice at Singer's back.

He planned this!

***

Nearly three more hours passed of riding bareback on the horse before we made it to a towering two-story inn. It looked like a giant abandoned estate from the way vines and other greenery grew over the expanse of it.

Is this a fairy inn?

"What is this place?"

"What does it look like?" I rolled my eyes, turning my gaze from Singer's back to the inn.

Noel continued to follow behind Singer and Shadow until we reached a stable to the right of the building with a few horses already settled inside. Singer slid off of Shadow before guiding him to a vacant pin. After he made sure there was a proper amount of hay and water for the stallion, he turned to me with an expectant look on his face.

"Well? Get off of Noel. Hasn't she suffered under your weight long enough?"

"Shut up, halfwit," I growled.

"I'm surprised you actually know what that word means." I huffed, deciding to be the bigger person and ignore him. You can't argue with an insane person, right?

Gingerly, I threw one leg over the side of Noel before sliding down. When my stiff legs hit the ground, they immediately buckled, sending me hurtling to the unforgiving ground. A pained groan left my lips.

"What's wrong? Not strong enough to stand on your own two feet?" Whirling my head in his direction, a burning flame of hate-filled my eyes.

"I would be if you had let me take a break from riding that horse for at least five minutes!"

"You were complaining about the breaks, so I assumed you didn't need them anymore."

"You're evil!"

"If I were evil, I would have pushed you off the horse and watched in delight as you fell or left you stranded out in the forest."

"Then you're an antagonist."

"I'll take it. Now get inside before the doors lock." With that said, he walked away towards the inn.

"Hey!" I yelled. He paused, slowly turning around with a smirk on his face.

"What?"

"Aren't you going to help me?"

"I thought you needed help finding answers, not help standing up."

Deep breaths… you still need his help… don't kill him.

Taking in one last deep breath, I placed both of my palms on the ground and pushed myself onto wobbly feet. When I didn't fall after a few seconds, I let out a sigh of relief.

"Don't forget to put Noel into a stable. On second thought, I'll do it. You'd probably forget to make sure she has everything she needs to survive the night."

That's it!

"How about I leave you out here and take the horses inside with me? They'll be far better company than you."

"As a matter of fact, I thought the same thing, except you, were the one staying out here." My glare intensified, turning my back on him. He guided Noel into the stall next to Shadow's, a chuckle leaving his lips.

"Shut up, you petulant child." His laugh sounded throughout the stables.

I followed closely behind Singer as he glided passed me. Walking to the front doors of the inn, Singer pushed them open revealing a large dining area filled with wooden tables and chairs. A large bar was along the expanse of the right wall while the left held two separate staircases leading to the upper level. Considering it was nearing nightfall, the dining hall was scarcely littered with a few faye- most of which I could tell were fairies. Keeping his eyes forward, Singer led the way to an empty table near the back. It was right next to the bar where a hooded man sat and within a stone's throw from the stairs. Pulling out one of the chairs, Singer gave me a leveled look.

"Stay here. Don't speak to anyone- don't even look at anyone. I will be right back." I grunted but did as he said and sat. However, Singer being the complete jerk that he is, couldn't leave well enough alone. "Good stray." He taunted, petting the top of my head before vanishing up the stairs. I glared at his retreating form, leaning back.

"I'm not a dog, idiot," I grumbled, glaring a hole into the middle of the table.

If I imagine hard enough, I can almost picture that's Singer's head.

"I wonder, what's a girl doing traveling with a guy she doesn't like?" The hooded man said from his place at the bar taking a sip of his drink. I grunted, pulling my arms closer to my body.

"Trust me, if I had a choice in the matter, I wouldn't be."

"So, he kidnapped you?"

"As if he would! That boy is more likely to kidnap someone to use as bait than to keep them around for any other reason."

"Sounds like you're speaking from experience."

"He has used me as bait three times already."

"Oh?" The stranger turned his body slightly so he could look at me from the corner of his eyes. I couldn't help but pause as I took them in. His eyes were an ethereal shade of dark blue with white lines running from the pupil to the outer rim. "And you let him?"

"It's not like I knew what he was doing." The man grunted before turning his gaze forward. He gulped down the remainder of his drink before he stood and sat down across from me.

"Sounds like you need new company. Now, what business does a human have in these forests?" My eyes lowered to the table, my hands clenching into tight fists.

"I want to know… I want to know why I'm alone." I whispered, but I knew he could hear me from the low hum he let out.

"And why is that?"

"My entire family- my father, mother, and brother were all taken from me a few months ago, and I don't know why. I tried searching for answers on my own, but the person who ordered their deaths has sent an assassin to get rid of me too."

"You don't say? That sounds like a rough time."

"The worst part is, I don't know why it happened- why it's still happening."

"Sounds maddening." He absently commented as a waitress made her way over to refill his cup.

"I wish I knew." Slightly shocked, he blinked at me a few times before resting his elbow on the table, his head leaning against the closed fist.

"Oh?"

"I wish that I knew why my family was taken from me." He took a sip of his drink before swirling the contents in the cup, his eyes never leaving me.

"Are you sure that is what you want?"

"With everything that I am." A sigh left my lips as I raised my head to give this random stranger a grateful smile. "Though it's not like you can do anything about it, but thank you for letting me ramble- Singer would never let me do this."

"I'm glad to be of service." He smirked before gulping down the rest of his drink before he stood up. "But, for future advice, you shouldn't tell people your wishes."

"Why not?"

"A wish is a powerful thing in these lands. Take heed to have some restraint in telling them." I blinked at him as a smirk spread across his lips.

Hasn't someone told me that before?

"Why? They're not valuable." Instead of responding, the man's smirk widened as he took out a small pouch and threw it onto the bar before heading to the door.

"Until next time… Jayde." My eyes widened as I whirled around only to see his retreating back.

How does he know my name?

"See you next time, Alastar." The barkeeper called, cleaning a wooden mug with a small cloth as the door closed behind the man. After a minute, my eyes finally drifted from the entrance to the barkeeper.

"Who was that?" The man glanced up at me before turning his eyes back down to the mug in his hands.

"A regular customer." He simply stated before turning his back to me to place the mug into a set of cabinets behind the counter. I opened my mouth to say something, but a hand on my shoulder nearly caused me to jump out of my skin.

"What did I tell you about talking to people?"

"What did your mother tell you about being nice?" I shot back as my heartbeat settled once again. He grunted, taking a step back.

"If you're done drawing attention to yourself, I got us a room for the night. That is unless you still want to sleep out in the stables while the horses enjoy the luxury of a warm bed." I scoffed brushing passed him, the smirk on his face visible from the corner of my eye. "So, are you going to lead the way to the rooms, or will you wait for me?" I rolled my eyes, taking in a deep breath.

You still need him… keep calm.

"By all means, take the lead." He let out a small chuckle as he walked up the staircase to the right. We made our way up and entered a large square walkway that wrapped around towards the other side. The middle of it was wide open, revealing the dining area below. A wooden railing lined the walkway creating a protective barrier for those moving around it.

"Try not to fall over the railing, stray." Singer teasingly called over his shoulder as he continued to walk by the doors lining the wall.

"Shut up, you rat," I growled back, crossing my arms over my chest. He grunted, stopping at the last door tucked into the corner. Twisting the knob, Singer opened the door before stepping aside to allow me to enter first. "So, you do have some knowledge of chivalry."

"Or I just know that strays have a tendency to run off, and I don't feel like hunting you down." I glared at him before going into the room. From what I was expecting, it's decent. Two full-sized beds, a dresser, a window, a door to what I think is a bathroom, a wardrobe, and a large window showing the setting sun along with the vast forest.

"It's bigger than what I thought it would be."

"That's because you're a spoiled brat." I shot him another glare before throwing my bag onto the closest bed. Just as I was about to sit on it, Singer scoffed. Rolling my eyes, I waited for the smart-mouth comment to come.

"I see, you want to be the first person the assassin sees if he decides to burst in and go ax murderer on us?" I whirled around and scowled at him before picking up my bag and tossing it on the other bed. "So, if he decides to burst through the window, you want to be scratched up with the glass?"

"Then what do you suggest, you insufferable fairy?"

"You're the one who can't decide on a bed." He sat down on the bed I was initially on, a giant smirk on his face.

"Oh, so you want to be the first one he sees?"

"You foolish stray, what are the possibilities that he finds us here?"

"But you said-"

"It's not my fault you're so gullible."

"You're such a jerk!"

"Why, thank you, stray." Letting out a loud huff, I flopped onto my bed, turning my back away from him. "You might want to go to sleep. We'll be going to my friend's home tomorrow." Instead of responding, I just closed my eyes and tried to block out all the sounds surrounding me.

***

"No!" The broken scream died on my lips, my back shooting from the bed, my mind in a haze of panic, and absolute terror. My eyes darted back and forth, searching for danger with blurry vision. A cold sweat clung to my body, making me feel sticky and dirty.

Another nightmare… thank goodness I can't remember it.

Placing a shaky hand on my forehead, I focused on breathing to calm my erratic heart.

"It was just a dream… just a dream."

"Does this happen every night?" A sharp intake of breath replaced the scream I almost let loose until my eyes connected to Singer lounging lazily against the windowsill.

"You nearly gave me a heart attack, Singer," I whispered, smoothing my sweaty hair back, letting out a deep breath.

"Does this happen every night?" He repeated.

"Most nights." Grunting in response, he turned his attention back out the window. Out of half curiosity and half desperation to forget the lingering terror still holding me hostage, I got out of bed and moved next to him. "What are you looking at?"

"The ogres." Partly surprised he answered me and didn't make some smart comment, I turned my gaze from him to look out as well.

Sure enough, within the canopy of the swaying trees, there were frightening monster with big round bellies and grotesque faces moving. They wielded large clubs that they used to smack the trees out of their path as they continued to travel. They moved quickly as if trying to get somewhere.

That's right, Singer said they have an allergy to sunlight.

"Can't they attack the inn?"

"You see, it's foolish questions like that that make you so annoying."

"Well, its responses like that that make you so insufferable." He turned his head to me, the moonlight giving him an almost ethereal glow, with that stupid smirk on his face.

"If you don't like my responses, then don't ask dumb questions." With that said, he got off the windowsill. Moving to his bed, he laid down with his back to me. "Try not to make too much noise. I'm a light sleeper."

"Good to know." I sarcastically threw back. A grunt was my only response before silence enveloped the room. An inaudible sigh left my lips as I took his place perched on the windowsill and looked out at the ogres. They began to disappear from my sight as they moved further away.

What was this nightmare about? Usually, when I wake up, the memory of all the horrors is still fresh as if it was still happening. Why can't I remember? Is there something different about this one?

Why am I so desperate to remember?

Closing my eyes, I let out another sigh before I rested my head against the cold glass of the window.

"I just wish I knew why this is happening…" I whispered to myself, a silent tear falling down my cheek.

"What did I say about the noise?"

"Shut up, you heartless harpy."

"Harpies don't live around here, foolish stray."

Seriously, how bad do I really need him?

***

"If we keep traveling at this speed, we should reach my friend's home before nightfall." Singer explained from his place on top of his horse. I let out a frustrated grunt as I shifted on top of Noel.

"Yeah, whatever." Just like yesterday, Singer is a complete maniac. For starters, he forced me to get up and on this blasted horse at the crack of dawn. Ever since then, we've been riding without a single brake. Considering that it was nearly six hours ago, and the sun is just about to go down, my legs are *killing me.*

How can he stand to be on his horse for so long?

As if sensing my thoughts, Singer pulled lightly on the mane of his horse coming to a standstill.

"You know," He started turning his head towards me. "We've been traveling for an awfully long time. Why don't we have a rest here for a while and continue in a bit? We're almost there anyway." I raised a brow.

Is he serious?

"There's even a pond near here that you can get freshwater and maybe even clean up a little." My eyes widened, my grip tightening in Noel's hair.

"Are you… being for real?" He rolled his eyes as he dismounted Shadow, petting the stallion's snout.

"Of course I am, you foolish stray. Now go before you lose your chance." Without even waiting for him to finish his sentence, I dropped from Noel and sprinted to the pond after Singer pointed out where the glorious water is.

In just two short minutes, the sight of the shining blue water came into view. My dry mouth watered as I ran to the pond, cupping my hand into the fresh stream. Taking a handful, I chugged it down greedily, repeating the motion at least six more times before finally satisfying my thirst. Waiting a few moments, I took out the water bottle from the pack Lilly gave me and dipped it into the water. Once it was full, I put the cap back on and placed it into the bag once again.

"Hello." My head snapped up as I looked around.

"Hello." raising a brow, I stood to my feet, slinging my sack over my shoulder. Just when I was about to run back to Singer, a movement in the water caught my eye. Looking down into the water, the face of a woman staring back at me sent my heart pounding a mile a minute.

"What?" Dropping my sack, I knelt by the pond getting close to the edge.

Is… is she alive?

Lifting my hand, I slowly reached out to see if I could touch her face or if it was just my dehydrated mind playing tricks on me. As my hand hovered over the water's surface, another covered in scales shot out from the pond, grabbing my wrist with an iron grip. A pair of arms wrapped around my waist and, with one forceful yank, we fell away from the water, the woman- or monster that grabbed me being dragged out.

"Well, how nice of you to show up." Singer greeted, reaching passed me to get a hold of the woman's arm that held me hostage.

The woman began to hiss as she tried to pull herself away to get back into the water. Using his other hand, Singer ripped off a scale causing the woman to shriek in pain before he let her go. The woman immediately retreated into the pond, hissing threateningly until she disappeared from sight. After examining the scale, he took out a small round container and carefully placed it inside, putting a comfortable distance between us once again.

"What…" He glanced at me with a small smirk on his face.

"That's what we call a siren. Unlike Hobbes and goblins, they live in water and are deadly if you're ever trapped in there with them. You really shouldn't get so close to the water next time."

"You didn't tell me there were carnivorous monsters in there!"

"I said you could get water and maybe get clean. If I had let that siren drag you into the pond, you'd have been very clean and refreshed."

"I swear, you're evil!"

"Only to humans."

"You're incorrigible!"

"Also correct. Would you like a prize?"

"No!"

***

By the time the sun was setting, we had arrived at Singer's friend's 'house'. In reality, his friend's 'house' is a giant estate that looks more like a small castle. There was no vegetation growing on it, nor were there any wooden material marring the structure. Everything was made from pure stone. As the sun set, the charcoal grey building let off a dull silver glow almost as if it was becoming the moon. There's even a large rock formation to the far left of the grounds that resembles a pair of open wings.

"Follow me." Singer said, leading the way to the rocks. As we grew closer, a small building came into focus. A few massive horses were inside along with a bottomless supply of hay and a small fountain.

"This is the stables?"

"What does it look like? A hot spring?" In my shock, I didn't even care to retaliate against the insult. Whoever Singer's friend is, they really cherish their horses.

After dismounting and caring for the horses, Singer led the way back around the large mansion towards the front door. Without even bothering to knock, Singer pushed the door open and walked right in. When he noticed my hesitation, he turned to me with a raised brow.

"Would you hurry up before an ogre comes and eats you?" Without wasting another moment, I rushed inside after him, the door closing slowly behind us.

"Do you always break into your friends' houses?" he ignored me, continuing down the grand corridor towards a set of towering twin doors at the rear of the room. Right next to it sat a grand staircase that winded up to five floors. A skylight overlooked it, all showing the soft spray of remaining sunlight from the setting sun.

"It's not breaking in if he knows I'm coming."

"But he didn't invite you in."

"Are you trying to tell me that you now believe in vampires? You're such a foolish stray." I opened my mouth to say something, but the sound of a massive metal object hitting the ground sent me flying towards his back, clinging to the fabric of his semi-tight shirt for dear life. He didn't comment. Although, the mocking snicker he released was proof enough that he was on the verge of letting out a string of insults.

Less than a minute later, we were standing in front of the intimidating set of doors. Without hesitating, Singer pushed the doors open, revealing a study that seemed just as large as the main entrance. The walls were made of bookshelves that reached high into the ceiling with a large desk and chair settled in the very back of the open space. Behind that lay a window that was slightly wider than the table but short enough that it left about a five-foot distance from the ceiling to the top of it. However, an eerie feeling settled in my gut when we *still* didn't see this friend.

"Singer?"

"What do you want now, stray?"

"Where is your friend?" He turned his head to me and opened his mouth to speak. Suddenly, the curtains to the window snapped shut, and the double doors slammed closed, casting the room into complete darkness. My grip on Singer's shirt tightened as I moved closer to him in fear.

"Singer?" The feeling of the fabric being snatched from my grasp sent a shot of panic through me.

"Singer!" A deep, echoing laughter sounded through the room.

A sensation of someone's breath on my neck sent me into a panic as I swung my fist back. When I hit nothing but air, fear raised up in the pit of my stomach. Just as quickly as the room became dark, the curtains opened, allowing the light of the rising moon to shine in the room. As my eyes adjusted, I saw Singer lounging casually in the chair behind the desk with his arms crossed and a smirk on his face.

"What's wrong, afraid of the dark?" He taunted, his smirk growing at my glare.

"Maybe, it is just afraid of monsters that may lurk in the darkness." My eyes snapped to the man sitting across from Singer. The man's back was towards me, but it looked slightly misshapen. It's like his shoulders were higher than they were supposed to be. His hair looked black at first, but as the moon shined more on it, it started to turn a beautiful shade of dark blue.

"Who are you?" I found myself whispering before I could stop myself. The man shifted in his seat before he began to stand. My eyes widened at the sight of his back once he fully rose.

Are… are those wings?

Sure enough, the twin pair of black feathery wings folded against his back fluttered slightly, showing that they were, indeed, real. He turned towards me, his shimmering yellow eyes that had an oval pupil similar to a cat staring straight through me. A smirk lay on his lips, sending a chill down my spine.

"Good evening, little human. My name is Favian, welcome to my home."

XI

"It's been a while since we last talked. How have you been? Eat any desperate housewives lately?" Singer passive-aggressively asked, leaning further back into the chair. Favian turned his entrancing gaze away from mine to look at Singer.

"I have been well, friend." He started settling back down into the chair he occupied seconds before. "And no, I have not had that luxury in quite some time. Though, that reminds me, how is your darling family?"

"They are absolutely lovely."

"… Ms. Lilly forced you to come, didn't she?"

"More like threatened torture in the most immoral fashion." The two laughed.

Weren't they just politely insulting each other?

Apparently, my confusion showed because Favian turned his head to examine me from the corner of his eye.

"What a delectable little human you have with you." He commented before turning his eyes back to Singer. "Why is she with you? Did you bring her here as a dinner offering?"

"No, in fact, my mother would castrate us both if you ate her."

"Then, who is she?"

"Ask her." Singer waved his hand in my direction before turning his gaze towards the left wall, scanning the books on it with a bored expression.

"Very well, then." Favian spun his chair around to face me. "Who are you, little human?"

"Jayde… Jayde Henryk." My eyes trailed over his form, taking notice of the black suit he wore with a white undershirt and his bird-like feet crossed at the ankle. "What kind of faye are you?" A crooked smile spread across his lips as he tilted his head to the side.

"Come closer, and I'll tell you, little Jayde." He raised his hand, beckoning me towards him. A strange feeling wrapped around my body practically screaming at me to go closer- to listen and do anything that he says, but I refuse to succumb to it. Instead, I shake my head to show I won't, taking a step back for extra emphasis. His chest rumbled before he let out a soft chuckle. "I like this human of yours. She's not as easily tempted as others." He whirled his chair back around, linking his fingers together underneath his chin. "Now, what do I owe the pleasure of your visit?" Instead of answering, Singer merely turned his eyes to me with an expectant look.

"Well? Tell him, stray." Anger bubbled up in the pit of my stomach.

Why can't he tell him? He's his friend!

"My family was murdered for a reason unknown to me, and now there is a man after me. Lilly told me that if I find the fairy queen, then she will tell me why my family was murdered and who did it." The room was silent. Favian's entrancing eyes bore straight through my soul before he folded his left arm in his lap while propping his other onto the armrest of the chair lying his head on his fist.

"This man sounds like an assassin and, judging from the way you seem more angry than sad, this journey sounds more like a revenge quest. Now, that begs the question, why would someone be vengeful towards a person that has done them no previous harm? From how you just explained it, that would make no sense unless this person after you is the man that murdered your family and is now after you to finish what he started. So, in short, an assassin is hunting you after being paid to murder your family. The person behind the scenes is waiting for confirmation that you're dead before going after what he really wants. However, you don't know what he wants, so you are seeking out the fairy queen to ask what was so important that your entire family must be dead before this person can get it?" A smirk formed on his lips at the sight of my jaw hitting the floor. My eyes widened to the size of saucers. "Am I right, little Jayde?"

"How did you-"

"Oh my- do you really think you're smart enough to outwit geniuses?" Singer called, giving me an incredulous look. I opened my mouth to speak, but no sound would come out.

"It seems your little human didn't want you to know that. Why is that, I wonder?"

"Who cares what her reasons were, she's a horrible liar. We all knew what was happening when she first told us the story."

"Then it was cruel of you to allow her to think she had you fooled."

"Then she shouldn't have tried to lie and get me into trouble with my mother."

"You sound like a scorned child." They continued to go back and forth with each other. Favian would nonchalantly mock Singer in his formal way of speaking while Singer continued to taunt me.

Hasn't he learned enough about me to gain some amount of sympathy!

Something within my mind seemed to break. A broken laugh left my lips, gaining both male's attention.

"Go ahead- keep taunting me! My feelings are far too numb to care anymore!" I hissed pacing back and forth. "Yes, the man chasing me *is* an assassin, and he *did* take my family away from me. Now he's after me, and I don't know *why*! My father wouldn't tell me, and I have no memory of something my family could have that would make someone want to get rid of all of us to get. None of this makes any sense to me, and, through some form of twisted dumb luck, I met Singer. I had hoped that maybe he could protect me from that maniac until I figured this whole thing out, but he ended up being another form of torture. I don't know what I did to deserve this treatment from him, and I don't know what I did to make him so annoyed with me, but all I ask is that he stop. Why can't he show me even the smallest bit of compassion and-" A hand pressing against my throat until my back hit the door cut off my rant. A sharp gasp fell from my lips as I stared into cold yellow eyes.

"Your tears do not soften my heart, little human, and nor will they soften the heart of a hungry beast prepared to rip you to shreds. No one will want to help you if you continue to cry like a defenseless child. Remember, in these woods, prey makes way for predators." His grip tightens slightly, not hard enough to choke but hard enough that it might leave a bruise. "Learn to be a predator, little human. Then, you may survive long enough to learn the answers you seek." With that said, he let me go. He stared at me for a moment longer before turning away and heading to the right wall, scanning over the books.

"I can help you find the fairy queen." Reaching his hand out, he pulled a leatherback book from the shelf and opened it reading a page. "But, I will require payment." He didn't glance up as he made his way to his desk. Singer stood from his seat and moved around the desk, allowing Favian to sit at the head.

"I have it for you." Singer said, taking out the vial and container from his pouch.

He tossed the materials onto the table before sitting down in the chair across from Favian. Setting his book on the desk, Favian reached out a hand taking the contents. He held them up in front of him before placing them back down. He flipped a few pages in his book before stopping on a page filled with small text. He turned his gaze up, motioning for me to come forward. Hesitantly, I walked towards the desk, sitting down in the chair next to Singer.

"You need to seek out one of the two ruling fairy regents."

"Two?" I asked quietly. Favian leaned back in his chair, his full attention on me.

"Yes, one monarch for the two types of faye- the Seelie and the Unseelie or in simpler terms, the good and the mischievous. If you can find one of them, then you will be able to get the answers you seek. It is a part of the rules of both the Unseelie and Seelie court that they must grant at least one wish a being makes. The only problem is that you must find them, and they're very elusive."

"Is there a difference between the two courts?" He tilted his head to the side, never breaking eyes contact.

"Of course. The monarch of the Seelie court is the fairy queen Ms. Lilly spoke of. She will grant you the information you wish to know. The monarch of the Unseelie court will grant you your wish as well, but it won't be in the way you wanted."

"What do you mean?"

"Imagine a man came to each of the monarchs and asked for untold riches. The fairy queen would grant him his wish, and he would leave the richest man in the world. On the other hand, the fairy king would grant him his wish, however, he would face cruel consequences. For example, the riches he possessed might result in his death either from jealousy or envy."

"Basically, you want to find the fairy queen and make your wish to her." Singer summarized, leaning back in his chair. I swallowed hard, my eyes glued to the desk in front of me. What if I find the fairy king? Is terrible happening afterward?

Yes.

"Where are they?"

"Only a person with clarity in their hearts can find them." I raised a brow, slowly lifting my gaze to meet his.

"What does that mean?" A smirk was my only response.

"It is my pleasure to extend a welcome for you two to spend the night in my home. After a goodnight rest, you two can continue on your journey refreshed and rejuvenated." He stood from his seat, straightening out his suit. He motioned for us to stand. "Please, follow me to your rooms." He stepped towards the door but paused. Turning to us, he kept his eyes on me. "I only have to ask that little Jayde stays in her room." I raised a brow prepared to ask why, but Singer placed a warning hand on my shoulder.

"The stray here can easily do that. I'm sure she's tired from all the wandering she's done anyway." Giving Singer a sideways look, I brushed his hand off of my shoulder.

"I can speak for myself!" I growled back at him. Favian let out a short laugh, the smirk returning to his lips.

"The little human is learning to be a predator. Maybe you will survive." With that, he turned around and pushed open the doors. We followed him through the foyer and up the stairs. As we ascended, a thought occurred to me.

"Singer?"

"What do you want, stray?" I shot him a look from the corner of my eye but let the comment slide for the moment.

"How are we going to find the fairy queen?"

"You're such a foolish stray." I glared at him elbowing him hard in the ribs. He grunted softly placing a hand over his bruised side.

Why is he such a jerk?

"Since you're too much of a jerk to answer that simple question, can you at least tell me where we are going after this?" He didn't even acknowledge me.

Is he ignoring me?

I was about to hit him again when he shifted closer to me.

"When we get there, don't stray from my side. I can't have you getting killed because you wanted to be a curious cat." I raised a brow.

What is that supposed to mean?

Before I could ask him, he quickened his pace leaving me straddling behind him in confusion.

***

I don't know if it is out of fear or an inability to sleep, but I found myself pacing the large room- or apartment to be accurate- that Favian gave me. With the nightmares becoming more lifelike and graphic, I find myself believing that my lack of sleep is more from fear than anything.

Maybe finding these answers will give me closure?

A sigh broke through my lips as I collapsed on the giant king-sized bed. It rested just below a wide window with two massive glass doors. Red curtains pulled to the side completed the simple yet elegant decor. Moonlight drenched the room warding off the darkness.

"I wonder what this fairy queen looks like," I whispered to myself, my eyes glued to the moon.

"Singer, it's been ages!" A female screamed in a tone that was borderline drunk.

Raising my eyebrows, I glanced at the door as the sounds of loud music came streaming through the creases.

Are they having a party downstairs?

Cautiously, I got out of my spot on the bed, making my way to the door. My heart pounded in my chest as Favian's words echoed through my head.

I only have to ask that little Jayde stays in her room.

Was he planning to throw a party? Is that why he didn't want me to leave the room?

Or is it because the guest would probably eat me?

"I see you don't act on impulse like most humans do, little Jayde." Nearly jumping out of my skin, I whirled around to see Favian lying tiredly on my bed. An arm was draped over his eyes while one of his knees was propped up.

"What's going on downstairs?"

"A party if the music and obnoxious yelling didn't clue you in."

"Why am I not allowed to go down?"

"Considering there are harpies, fairies, and other faye down there that will not hesitate to turn you into a stew, I have arranged so you will stay here where it is safe."

"I can take care of my-" Before I could blink, my back was smashed against the wall. Favian stared down at me with calculating yellow eyes, his right arm pressed against the door above my head.

"I would tell you that you would be sadly mistaken. I've told you before, out here, prey like you make way for predators like Singer and me. You are only alive through the good graces of Ms. Lilly. Be grateful and do as you're told." He removed his arm and made his way to the window, pushing the doors open.

"At least I'm brave enough to walk among you without fear!" My heart pounded in my ears as he slowly turned towards me. A laugh broke through as a sly smirk found its way to his lips.

"I like you, little Jayde Henryk." And with that, he jumped out of the window. His wings spreading out, allowing him to glide through the air like a bird.

XII

"It has been a pleasure having you two," Favian said as he leaned against the rock wall of the entrance to the stables. I stood by Noel, petting her long snout as Singer made sure the saddles and reigns that Favian loaned us were secure on both horses.

"Fantastic, please don't tell my mother we were here."

"May I ask why?"

"Because she'll think I was trying to feed the stray to you for dinner and will hunt me down." Favian's chest rumbled as he nodded his head.

"I will keep your secret if you can do a favor for me as well." Singer nodded his head in a show that he was listening. "Teach little Jayde to defend herself. If she stays solely dependent on you, she may very well get you killed." Pausing as he finished his work, Singer strained his neck to make eye contact with his friend.

"I'll try, but the stray may end up falling on any weapon I give her with her level of coordination." Favian's smile widened, coming closer to me. He knelt beside me, holding his laced his fingers near my feet. Placing my foot into his hands, he pushed me upwards. Swinging my leg over the side of Noel, I grabbed on to the newly applied reigns to steady myself.

"Remember, little Jayde, prey make way for predators." Favian quietly told me before stepping away from the stallion. Singer slung himself quickly onto Shadow taking the reins in his hands. Shadow moved around a little, getting used to the new weight on his back before settling down.

"See ya later, old friend," Singer called before snapping the reins jolting the horse forward. On instinct, Noel followed the male stead's actions and sprung into a sprint right behind him.

While the wind blew through my hair, sending it into a wild dance behind me, Favian's words still rung in my head. If I don't learn how to defend myself, then Singer may die? Isn't he strong enough to protect himself from anything, though? My eyes raised to look at the back of the person charged to defend me.

I won't let another person die because of me.

Nodding my head firmly, I allowed the thought to swirl in my head for a moment longer before engraving it in my brain. Yes, no one else will die because of me- not if I have anything to do with it.

"Singer!" I called before I could stop myself.

Why am I calling him?

Hearing his name, he pulled back on the reins slowing our pace to a steady trot allowing our horses to walk side by side.

"What?" He asked in a borderline pleasant tone.

Where'd all the taunting go?

"How was the party?" I asked quickly.

"I could explain it to you, but since you are a difficult human who doesn't know anything, I'm not going to waste my breath."

There it is.

"For your information, I've been to many parties before, and I think I know a little-" Singer veered his horse in front of mine, bringing Noel to a standstill.

"This 'party' is nothing like a human social gathering. These are meant for Faye to gorge themselves on violence and flesh." He sat straighter, his eyes still harshly glaring at me. "If they had found you, they would've killed you." My eyes widened before I diverted them to examine the reins in my hands.

"Why would Favian have the party then?"

"He didn't have a choice. It's just my luck his lovely neighbors caught your scent before we could hide you in the manor. Lucky for you, we were able to convince them I had a stash of humans they could have. Well, if they could kill me first." snack." My heart dropped. This happened because of me?

"She may very well get you killed."

"Are you okay? I mean, I can't have my bodyguard injured." I added quickly, turning my gaze up to meet his. He huffed, pulling on his horse's reins, so his face was out of my line of sight.

"I'm the amazing Singer, what do you think?" I lowered my gaze slightly, a small smile forming on my lips. So, in other words, he's telling me he's okay.

Good.

"We'll be reaching the next inn in a couple of hours. After that, we can brainstorm on how to achieve clarity. Well, more like how to make you achieve it. That in itself will take us months if not years." He snapped the reins on his horses back, sending Shadow into a slow trot once again. Noel started forwards right behind him.

About an hour passed, and we were still traveling in uncomfortable silence. It felt as if something was hanging in the air between us that needed to be said. Is it something that Singer needs to tell me? Then what could it be?

I don't care what it is- I can't take this anymore!

"Why did you bring Favian goblin nails and a Siren's scale?" I blurted out.

"He uses them to make a perfume that can numb the mind."

"Why does he need it?"

"Favian is a meat-eater. His favorite type is desperate women. I'm going to let you fill in the blanks." I thought about it for a second before realization dawned on me.

He must use it to lure in his victims.

A queasy feeling filled me.

How long does he keep them in his house before he eats them?

"What's your favorite food?" The much needed distraction diverted my thoughts from what was about to cross my mind. Glancing at me over his shoulder, Singer raised a confused brow.

"What?"

"My favorite food is turkey." Noel's loud shriek of pain deafened me before I was sent flying over her head, landing with a loud thud on my back.

I groaned in pain before I felt another body landing next to me and the distant shout of another shriek coming from Shadow. Cracking my eyes open slightly, the sight of Singer lying stationary on his back, his eyes towards the clouds, took over my vision. Twisting my body, I started to get up, but a massive net falling from the trees on top of me knocked me back down to the dirt. Before I could even think about escaping, the unrelenting need to sleep turned my limbs to jelly.

"Sleeping powder." Was the soft murmur I heard from Singer before darkness took over my vision.

***

A soft moan left my lips as my heavy eyes finally opened, the dreamless sleep I was put into soon forgotten as terror took hold. Shooting to a sitting position, I noticed the warm blanket falling into my lap and the cozy bed beneath me. Scanning the room, I noticed I was in a wooden caravan with a single window to my left that let in the afternoon sunlight.

Where's Singer?

"Singer?" I whispered when I couldn't find him. Panic set over me when I didn't get a response. "Singer?" I called louder.

Did Hawk find us?

"Your friend is fine, Jayde Henryk." The familiar female voice called as the door to the caravan opened. Dove stood before me in a white blouse and a dark purple skirt that draped to her feet where a set of bells laid against both her ankles. "How are you?"

"Where is he?" I demanded, getting out of bed and into a fighting stance. If I had to fight her to find Singer, then so be it- at least I'll go down swinging!

"He is in the caravan across from us. Would you like to see him?" She gently explained with an amused smile on her face. I nodded, lowering my fists but keeping my guard up.

Turning on her heels, she led me out of the caravan. The sunlight blinded me for a moment before we continued the short journey across the ample deserted space. Six similar caravans were organized in a that created a crescent shaped courtyard. Pausing at the door, she knocked softly before motioning for me to walk in first. Eyeing her for a moment, I went inside in much more of a hurry, then I should be considering my relationship with the fairy. All the same, I was desperate to see if he was okay.

Looking around the room, I found him lying shirtless on a cot elevated a couple feet off the floor. His left side was covered in a smooth green paste, splotches of red-violet staining the white sheets he laid on, which I could only assume was fairy blood.

They hurt him!

Whirling around, a fiery blaze of anger covering my eyes.

"What did you do to him?"

"Stop being so loud, you screeching stray." Turning back around, the sight of Singer sitting up slowly sent a wave of relief over me, washing away my anger.

"You're okay," I whispered.

"We didn't harm him. We just treated his wounds," Dove explained, crossing her arms under her chest and leaning against the door frame. Glancing at her for a second, I turned my gaze back to Singer, a thought filling my mind.

The party…

Moving closer to Singer's bedside, I allowed my hand to hover over his wound.

"You got this from the party, didn't you?" I mumbled.

"The fairy that landed the hit has a bigger hole in his stomach." He scoffed, plopping back down, closing his eyes as if he were exhausted.

He should be- he deserves to take a break for a while.

"We should leave him to rest, don't you think?" Dove called. I nod, turning away from Singer and walking out of the caravan when his voice firmly called out.

"Remember, nomad, I have eyes everywhere." Dove glanced back at him nodding her head.

"Of course, fairy." Singer grunted before his breath began to even out, signaling he was drifting off to sleep. Dove smiled, closing the door softly behind her. When Dove came close to me, she motioned for me to follow her as she began to walk away. Hesitantly I fell into step beside her.

"What is this place?"

"This is a temporary campsite my people have set up." She answered without missing a beat.

"Where are they?"

"They are in the main square. Where we came from is the medical center."

After a minute, the sounds of laughing children and the loud chatter of a large crowd filled my ears. As the sounds grew louder, I could see over two dozen more caravans. They were situated in four different semi-circles of six creating a ring around a large fire pit. Women, children, and men bustled about doing various chores like cleaning laundry in a river settled on the far right of the camp, sharpening tools, or skinning and preparing food. Others merely lounged about, either playing music or gossiping while children weaved in and out playing.

"Follow me," Dove said, moving in the direction of the river. Once we reached it, she settled down on the moisten dirt, waiting patiently for me to sit as well. When I did, she leaned back, staring at the water. "You may ask me any question you'd like."

"Why were you at my philosophy class?" A playful smirk danced on her lips.

"I would think, with all that's happened, you would've forgotten something as insignificant as that."

"Everything feels like it happened yesterday." She hummed softly turning her gaze to the sky.

"I was watching you and your family."

"Why?"

"I was ordered to."

"By who?"

"Someone you will meet soon." I sighed, turning to the river.

"How long have you been watching me?"

"From that day to when you entered the forest." My head snapped in her direction.

"So you were there when my father was…" *killed.* The word just wouldn't leave my lips as the day replayed in my mind.

"Yes, along with five others. We were the ones who saved you, but we weren't able to get there fast enough to save your father." I turned my gaze back down towards the water. Why can't I get angry at her for not being able to save him?

Maybe it's because you now know that some people can't be saved.

"Though I can't tell you why all of this has happened to you, I may be able to shed some light on who this Hawk person is."

"Any kind of information will help," I whispered in response.

"I think that he is an ex-assassin who is now a mercenary. Why he became one, I have no idea."

"Why do you think he's a mercenary?"

"Assassins don't usually harm children." I hummed softly, an image of Aric coming to the forefront of my mind painfully constricting my chest. "Judging by the way he knew exactly where each member of your family would be that night, I can only assume that the person who ordered this is someone close to your family. The chances of this person doing this for money is highly unlikely. However, he definitely did this to gain or find something he couldn't if someone from your family was alive. In my opinion, the massacre is mostly to make sure that no one will be able to turn him into the guard." I stayed quiet, allowing her words to sink in.

"Do you know what my family has that someone would have to kill us all to get?"

"I'm not entirely sure, but whatever it is, it is worth the price." I nodded, closing my eyes.

That's exactly what I thought.

"Just to help you think of some possible people who could be behind this, I think the person worked closely with your father." My eyes slowly moved to hers.

"What makes you think that?"

"Before your father was found, he was speaking of someone he knew betraying him." I nodded, remembering the night I spent barricaded in my room.

"Why would someone close to my father do something like this?"

"My guess is that your father may have purposefully or accidentally shown them something precious that's a family heirloom. They must have tried to take it beforehand before realizing that the only way to get it is if the entire Henryk family was gone first." I closed my eyes tightly before pulling my knees to my chest and burying my head into my folded arms.

So, he did do something to cause this.

"Can you please leave me alone for a while?"

"Are you sure you'll be okay?"

"Yes… I just… need to be alone." I said, slowly trying hard to keep my voice from shaking. She sighed softly before I heard her clothes rustling.

"Don't stay out here too late. It will be dark soon." The sounds of her retreating footsteps were all I needed to hear before I allowed the wall holding back the despair and anguish crash down. My shoulders shook violently, knocking me to the ground. I curled into a ball and cried. Burying my face in my hands, I muffled my sobs.

What could my family possibly have that someone would want? I've asked myself that question over a million times, and I *still* don't have an answer to it.

What did my father do to cause this?

Knowing what I know now, it couldn't have been a deal gone wrong or someone he wronged wanting revenge. No, this is for *something*, but what is it? There is no trinket that my family has that is valuable enough to warrant a death sentence for someone to get it. So what could it be?

"I just want to know." I sobbed to myself. Black spots dotted my vision before sleep hurtled me into a series of nightmares.

XIII

Light, happy laughter woke me. My eyes slowly opened, forcing the darkness that held me hostage throughout the night to retreat. Thankfully, the memory of the endless nightmares that plagued me was gone, making way for a blank slate. Slowly, I sat up, noticing that I was inside of a caravan.

Dove must have sent someone to carry me back.

I absently thought before getting up and walking outside. The sunlight immediately assaulted my eyes, forcing me to look away to allow them to adjust.

"Catch me if you can, Karlie!" A little girl shouted running past me, followed by another with features I can't ever forget.

Is that... Is that Karlie? Ginger's granddaughter? What is she doing out here?

Sure enough, the little girl with red pigtails I met in Redmage tackled the other girl to the ground, both erupting into a fit of laughter.

"Karlie?" I called. She paused, turning her bright brown eyes up to me, confused. After a second, a happy smile broke through her lips as she scrambled to her feet, running at me.

"Ella!" She cried, bounding into my arms. She laughed in my ear before pulling back, holding a hand to her mouth. "Oops, I mean Jayde." She smiled at my shocked face.

"What are you doing here? Where's your grandmother?"

"I'm not really an old woman, juvenile." A familiar voice called behind me. I turned to see a pretty woman with dark red hair and jaded blue eyes make her way over. The blue skirt she wore swayed with every step she took.

"Auntie Ginger!" Karlie exclaimed with a cheeky smile. She wiggled out of my grasp to run towards the woman.

"G-Ginger?" She lifted her eyes from the little girl who wrapped her arms around her torso to meet my shocked gaze.

"Yes, it's me, *Ella.*" She teased.

"How- what-?"

"I'm a nomad who specializes in espionage. I was asked to stay in Redmage to watch over you until we could figure out a way to get you and your father here without blowing our cover."

"Why was Karlie there?"

"I was teaching Karlie the art of disguise."

"How… old are you?" a soft laugh left her lips.

"Twenty-three." I nodded absently, the conversation I had with Dove yesterday suddenly making an appearance at the forefront of my mind.

"If you were there… then do you know that… Patrick…" Her face twisted for a split second before she turned away.

"I know." She whispered. Karlie looked up at her aunt's face and took her expression as her queue to leave, running over to the other children. "Patrick… he was… in disguise like me. He was supposed to get Ethan out of Redmage when we found out that the assassin was in town. Before that, he was only there to be a doctor for faye." I nodded content with just listening. "I was originally assigned to guard him, but a few months later, you and your father arrived." My eyes drifted to the side, a sadness filling me.

So, it was my fault he was killed?

"Hey, stray, where have you been?" We both looked behind me to see Singer walking towards us, a small red-violet splotch on the left side of his shirt were his injury lie.

"Singer, are you sure you should be moving around so soon?"

"My body is tougher than humans." His dark purple eyes shifted over to Ginger. "Who is this human?"

"My name is Ginger." He blinked, not saying a word.

Awkward...

"I think I should go check on Karlie. I will see you later, Jayde, Singer." with one final glance at the both of us, Ginger brushed past us going off to find the little red-haired girl.

"You know, you could have said something nice to her."

"And you could leave me alone, so I can get back to my life, but that ain't happening either." Rolling my eyes, I crossed my arms under my chest, shooting him a stern look.

"Ginger has just lost a close friend, and you come along making her feel-"

"Pause," he cut in returning my serious look. "Whatever you are about to explain has nothing to do with the list of problems my mother is forcing me to fix. Which brings me to one of the major problems on that list." He motioned for me to follow him as he began walking into the dense tree line surrounding the camp.

"And what would that be?" I asked, following just to see what he wanted.

After all, he did almost die for me.

"You, little annoying stray, need to learn how to defend yourself or at the very least, to give the impression that you can."

"I *can* take care of myself." Stopping midstride, he whirled around, an annoyed scowl on his face.

"Yeah, I've seen your version of taking care of yourself. Be grateful my mother is forcing me to take care of you; otherwise, you'd have been dead. Honestly, I've never seen someone lose so badly to a hobbe- of all things!" He added in a mumble turning back around to continue walking.

"Be grateful that my mother is forcing me to take care of you, nuh." I mocked, making a face at his back.

"I heard that you little stray."

"I'm glad you did." He snorted, stopping once again. Glancing around, he nodded his head as if satisfied before turning to me.

"Since you are a hopeless stray and I would like to get back to my life as soon as possible, I will teach you how to defend yourself."

"And how do you plan to go about that?" A smirk appeared on his lips as he bent down and picked up a small rock.

"By first showing you what you're dealing with when it comes to fairies." Without warning, he flicked the rock at me, hitting me right in the stomach. The force of the blow knocked me on my back, the wind leaving my lungs.

Ouch!

Lying still, I waited until I caught my breath long enough to sit up. Right when I did, the face of a red fox invaded my vision.

"What?" I blinked at it for a second as it just sat calmly in front of me *with an annoyed glint in its eyes?* Looking closer, I gasped.

Its eyes are purple!

"Singer?" The fox snorted, jumping away from me before its body began to morph and distort. A loud pop sounded before Singer was standing before me with his arms crossed. "How did you do that?" I gasped, scrambling to my feet.

"All advance fairies can shapeshift into two animals. That means you can't let your guard down- especially around wild animals. I don't need you getting killed because you wanted to pet a fairy disguised as a rabbit or something" He scoffed, not looking at me. A piercing scream silenced any other questions I had. My heart dropped as I turned my attention towards the camp. Black smoke billowed just above the area.

"Someone is attacking!" Without thinking, I began to run towards the camp. Could it be that Hawk knows I'm here? Is he punishing the nomads for helping me? The smiling faces of the families in the field- the happy faces of my family- flashed in front of me. Hawk's dagger dripping in blood rammed into my conscious propelling my feet to go faster.

I have to save them!

"Wait, you foolish stray!" Singer snapped, gripping my wrist, keeping me firmly planted to the ground.

"Let me go!" I screamed, trying hard to rip my wrist out of his grip, but he just wouldn't budge!

"What do you expect to accomplish going to them? You're far too weak to help." He used his opposite hand to pat me on the back. "Why don't you just run and save yourself?" Red tinted my vision as I snatched my arms from his grip in one powerful tug.

"You're a heartless jerk!" I screamed in his face before taking off towards the camp.

I won't run away from that cretin anymore!

In a matter of seconds, I was back in the camp. All around, the caravans blazed with roaring flames that threatened to spread to the trees surrounding the field. People scurried around frantically with buckets, baskets- anything they could fill with water- tossing the clear liquid on the flames. Immediately, I ran to a little girl who was struggling to carry a bucket filled with water and took it from her.

"Help people get out of here, I'll take care of this." She looked at me with wide, frightened eyes before nodding and running off. Faster than I've ever moved, I carried the bucket to the nearest caravan and dumped all of its content on the flame. After six more trips and the help of one other male, the fire was gone, *but there were half a dozen more.*

Everyone in the camp worked tirelessly. Everyone sprinted back and forth from the river to the burning caravans dumping as much water as they could onto the flames. An hour passed, and there was only one remaining caravan with a dimming fire. With one final bucket of water, the flame died out. Just like that, everyone felt the ability to breathe come back, a sigh of relief filling the destroyed camp.

"Thank goodness." I breathe, falling to my knees, panting. My arms shook from exhaustion, and my legs felt numb with the constant running and high stress.

How did this happen?

Just like that, another scream was heard followed closely by a gunshot that sent everyone into an uproar.

"Everyone evacuate!" A male hollered.

Immediately, people began to run in one direction leading away from the camp, screaming in panic. With a new wave of adrenaline, I got to my feet scanning the area in a frenzy. Through the trees behind the scattered crowd, I could see a small army, boots pounding the ground, announcing their presence. My pulse drummed in my ears as a few nomads wielding different weapons from swords to daggers created a defensive line between the soldiers and the escaping group. Among them, Dove's soft features stood out.

"Dove!" I shouted, moving towards her. She snapped her head in my direction, her grip on the lance she wielded tightening.

"Jayde, what are you still doing here? Run!" She shouted, pointing in the direction the crowd was disappearing to with her lance.

"I can help!"

"No, you can't!" A battle cry interrupted our dispute as the soldiers broke through the tree line entering the camp. The nomads immediately charged, swinging their weapons with all their might taking out as many soldiers as they could before they were cut down. Dove cursed in a soft growl turning towards the soldiers, gripping her lance with both hands. "Grab a weapon or run, just don't die!" and with that, she lunged into the fray.

I watched in amazement as she swung her lance like a bat taking down dozens of the soldiers at a time. It was then that I was able to figure out, *these men are mercenaries.*

Why are they attacking a nomad camp?

A scream from one of the mercenaries charging at me cut off my thoughts. I barely dodged the attack, rolling to the side. The man gave me a crooked grin holding his jagged sword in front of him.

"Well, aren't I lucky that I get to kill such a pretty girl?"

"In your dreams, peasant!" I sneered. The man's ugly smile twisted into an angry scowl.

He growled, lunging with deadly precision. Hitting the dirt as the sword would have pierced my heart, I rolled away from him. Snatching a rock from the ground, I whirled around, chucking it as hard as I could at the back of his head. The man grunted in agitation before turning with a blazing fire in his eyes.

"Come here, you little runt!" He went to lunge at me, but a dark shadow dropped from the sky between us, slamming into the ground, creating a shockwave that shook the Earth, forcing everyone to their knees. Once the dust settled and the ground stilled, Singer stood amid the destruction scanning the battlefield with tired eyes.

"Singer?" I called, unsure. He glanced at me, smirked, put a hand over his chest, and fell to the ground. "Singer!" I hollered in frustration.

Did he just fake pass out in the middle of a battle? What is he doing!

Before I could get to him, a mercenary snatched my arm, twisting it painfully behind my back.

"Be good." He mocked, dragging me over to the other remaining nomads that were left standing- six in total, including Dove.

Like the others, the man bound my hands together, forcing me to my knees beside Dove. Two other mercenaries dragged Singer's limp body- faking or not- beside me. After testing to see if he was awake by slapping his face a little bit, they deemed him unconscious enough to not need binding. After that was done, all seventeen remaining soldiers stood before us, smirks and smiles of victory painting their faces.

"Thank you, men, you have been a huge help in my campaign." My eyes widened, my head snapping up to meet the eyes of the man who spoke.

It can't be...

The green eyes of the man who was my father's closest consultant and beloved family friend, Layne Pierce, stared wildly back at me.

"Uncle Layne?" His delirious eyes turned to me, a disgusting smirk on his lips.

"I'm not your uncle, heart breaker."

"Why are you doing this? These people haven't done anything!" His smirk only widened. He came closer, kneeling, so we were eye to eye.

"Oh, dear little Jayde, you really think it makes a difference if they have done something? They merely have something that I want, and I will do whatever it takes to get it." He leaned closer. "Just like how I got rid of your family." My heart stopped beating, my eyes grew larger. He leaned back, his smirk becoming more sinister.

"It was you?" I breathe.

"What can I say? Your father denied me what I wanted. I did what I had to." I lunged, fully intending to punch the smirk right off his face before murdering him but a mercenary stopped me. No matter how hard a thrashed and fought, the brutes grip never wavered.

"You were family! You taught me how to walk- you were there when my brother was born- how could you do this to us?" I screamed, tears spilling down my cheeks.

"It's simple, the only way I can get what I want is if your bloodline no longer exists. You are the last living Henryk, as of such, all I have to do is kill you."

"But why- what is so important that you have to do this?" He opened his mouth to speak, but a loud yawn from Singer cut him off.

No- he was about to tell me!

"So, the fairy has awoken," Layne noted rising to his full height, looking down his nose at Singer as he sat up. Singer scoffed casually, leaning back like he wasn't being held hostage.

"Gee, what gave you that impression?"

"Excuse me?" a dark aura surrounded Layne. Singer either didn't notice or didn't care.

"You must be as dumb as the stray or as blind as an ogre if you didn't catch the immense sarcasm I just threw at you." A crazed glint flashed through Layne's eyes. Yanking out a dagger tied to his hip, he lunged at Singer. Moving at the same time, Singer shifted enough so the blade pierced his right shoulder instead of his chest.

"Singer!" I cried as he fell in a heap. Layne stood up, his hair a mess and his breathing labored. He looked at the blood, beginning to pool around Singer's body before letting out a demented laugh.

"Kill them! Kill them all!" He shrieked, his voice filled with bloodlust.

My heart pounded in my chest as the mercenaries advanced towards us, their weapons held up ready to strike.

No!

Tears slid down my cheeks as I struggled hard against my bindings.

I won't die here- I need to find out why!

A dark shadow cast overhead bathing us in darkness.

"What is this?" Layne shouted, turning his gaze up. All eyes widened at the sight of dozens of harpies circling above us, hissing threateningly.

"Harpies!"

"Run!" The mercenaries shouted in a panic as they ducked in fear. Layne glared at the men pulling out a pistol from his belt.

"No one is going anywhere!" He roared. The ground began to rumble before a horde of goblins and Hobbes broke through the tree line sprinting full speed towards the terrified mercenaries. Just at that moment, arms wrapped around my waists before a pulling sensation came over me, distorting my vision.

"Don't move, stray." Was the last thing I heard before my vision went white.

"Let go of me!" I screamed, clawing at the hands that held me. Singer released me, but kept a tight grip on my wrist. I glared at the offending appendage before yanking my arm, trying to escape. "Let me go! I have to go back and help them!" With a grunt, Singer let go of my arm, causing me to stumble.

"You can try and find them, but we're too far away for you to find your way back." Anger boiled inside of me.

"You idiot!" I cried, shoving him.

"All of those people are going to die now!" He merely blinked. A bellowing laugh soon followed.

"You foolish stray, that was merely an allusion spell."

"What?" His smirk only widened at my bewilderment.

"The goblins were a herd of wild horses I spelled months ago just in case I was ever in a situation where I needed a distraction."

"What about the harpies?"

"Birds that Favian owns- also cloaked with an illusion spell."

"Why didn't you tell me?" I shoved him again, this time harder than before. When he only stumbled back a step, my frustration grew.

"Please, you know as well as I do that if I did you would have blown the secret in your irrational fit of panic. On the other hand, I love to toy with your emotions." My jaw almost hit the floor, but I caught myself, closing my eyes tightly.

How many times has he done this? Five? Hasn't he always had some kind of ridiculous over the top plan to fix everything?

Why should I work myself up over this stuff anymore?

"What's wrong? Cat got your tongue, little stray?"

"Shut up." I snapped, shooting him a nasty glare before turning away, a sigh escaping my lips. "Will… will the nomads at least be okay?"

"That's not up to me."

"What do you mean?"

"Whether they survive or not is on them. I may have gotten the mercenaries and that insane man off their scent, but they're not my problem anymore. My mother is only forcing me to look after you." Letting out a short snort, he strolled passed me.

My hand twitched to snatch him back and demand clarification, but the more levelheaded part of me held me still. He's always made sure that everything was okay in the end. He's even sacrificed his own health twice already. With another sigh, I followed behind him, keeping my glare at ground level to keep the urge to punch him at bay.

Now that I think about it, what is Singer planning? When I first met him, he used me for bait to catch a hobbe, then a goblin, a siren, to draw Favian out, and now to cast these weird illusions. I know he was using the goblin hair and siren scale to pay Favian for the information we needed, but what about the other stuff? Why was he looking for a Hobbe's hair in the first place? Why did he have those horses spelled to look like Hobbes and goblins? Now that I think about it, who is Singer *really*? I'm positive that, no matter how terrifying his mother, maybe, there is no way he is solely helping me just because she told him too. What is he planning?

"Keep up, stray!" A grunt was the automatic response I gave before continuing.

"Where are we going anyway?"

"Keep your eyes open and mouth shut, then you'll figure it out."

"Or you could stop being a jerk and tell me."

"I'd rather the former."

"Why can't you stop being difficult and do the latter?"

"Well, it looks like we're at a standstill then."

"You know what I meant!"

"We're still walking, you foolish stray." A frustrated huff left my lips.

Why is he so stubborn! The sudden feeling of my face smacking into something hard silenced my rant and bruised my nose. Taking a step back, rubbing my sore nostrils, I glared at Singer's back.

"Why are we stopping?"

"You may be eager to jump off another cliff, but I'm not." Ignoring him, I moved passed him prepared to keep walking, but the sight of the steep drop off sent me scrambling back. I caught my breath, looking passed the cliff at the forest that stretched out further than I could see.

"Where are we?"

"On a cliff, foolish stray."

Inhale… exhale.

"Okay, where are we going then?" Singer smirked then shrugged.

"I don't know." His smirk grew into a crooked grin as he took a few steps back before running full speed at me.

"What are you doing?" I screamed. His arms wrapped around my waist before he sprang off of the cliff. The ground loomed threateningly beneath us.

He's trying to kill us!

In the next second, Singer's back hit the side of the cliff. He let me go causing us both to slide down the hill, him having the time of his life while I screamed in terror. After what felt like hours, we finally came to a stop at the bottom.

"Well, that was fun!" Singer laughed, getting up and dusting himself off. "Do you want to do it again?" I didn't even spare him a glare, my eyes still glued to the blue sky above me.

My heart, still banging painfully against my chest. A shadow cast itself over me. It took me a second to realize it was Singer's smirking face.

"Why are you still lying on the ground? Are you waiting for me to carry you?" To my surprise, there was no automatic response that I would usually give. With a sigh, I pushed myself off the ground and dusted myself off. Without even batting an eyelash, Singer stood up to his full height, stretched his arms out, and let out a long sigh giving me a wide smile. "So, where are we headed?"

"What?" My head whirled to him in utter disbelief.

Please tell me he did not just say that…

"Did the fall make you deaf, stray?"

"How am I supposed to know where we're supposed to be going?" His smile reduced to a mocking smirk.

"'Only a person with clarity in their hearts can find the fairy monarchs.' Isn't that the information you suffered a creepy night at a harpy's mansion to get?"

"You don't even know what that means!"

"I do, you don't."

"Then explain it to me?"

"Idiot, you need to know exactly what you want from them. They're not going to appear to you if you have a hundred wishes you want them to grant- it's not going to happen!"

"I do know what I want," I grunted, brushing passed him. If he wants me to lead the way- then I'll get us both lost!

"Then enlighten me."

"I want to know why my family was murdered."

"…I can't tell if you're lying or just plain naïve." Anger boiled deep within me. Twirling on the balls of my feet, I gave the heartless fairy a nasty glare.

"Then, tell me what I want!" I screamed, the feeling of hot tears trickling down my cheeks, shocking me. He blinked blankly before closing his eyes, a smirk on his face.

"I see, you're not just naïve, but foolish as well." He walked closer to me and flicked my forehead leaving a small bruise. Anger, confusion, depression, and, to my utter horror, amusement washed over me all at once, like a tidal wave. "Now lead the way, you stray cat." Being in the complete emotionally wrecked state I'm in, I just mechanically turned around and began aimlessly walking.

***

We walked for three more hours. I know that much because the sun started to descend passed the horizon. The lower it went, the more fear I felt.

"You do know that the ogres come out when it gets dark, right?" Singer is only adding to that fear. "I mean, if ogres attack, I'll be perfectly fine but you… you might as well say goodbye to ever finding the fairy monarchs. How well do you think you'd taste to a carnivore?"

"Shut up." I snapped, stopping in place.

There has to be a path to a town somewhere, right?

To the left? Nothing. To the right? A bunch of trees. In front? More trees!

"You're a hopeless stray!" Singer bellowed, thoroughly jolly in the presence of my despair. Without waiting for me, he began walking towards the right, moving the branches out of his way as he went.

"Hey- wait!"

He knows where shelter is, right?

Running behind him, I shoved the branches he let go of- in hopes they would smack me in the face I might add- until we came to a small clearing with a cottage on the very edge covered in vegetation. Actually, it looks very similar to Singer's house. Without wasting a second, Singer began strolling towards it like he owned the place. Reaching out, I grabbed his arm and snatched him back. Raising an amused brow, Singer gave me a once over.

"What- too scared?"

"You don't know who may live there! What if they're ogres or Hobbes or something else?" His lips quivered before he burst into laughter.

"They live underground or in caves- what would they do with a house?" He laughed before, once again, making his way towards the cottage. I tried to grab him, but he moved out of my range.

"Singer!" I whispered tiptoeing quickly behind him, keeping my head low to not make my presence known to whoever may lurk inside.

"Stop your crying, stray. It's vacant anyway." He called, placing a hand on the door handle.

"How do you know that?" He glanced at me as he pushed open the door.

"Because it's my house." I blinked as he disappeared inside. A few minutes later, light illuminated the entire place showing that this is a smaller version of the home he lives in now.

This place looks oddly similar to the cottage my father and I stayed in at Redmage. There was a small kitchen and a living room set up exactly like the one in Singer's current home. To the right of the door was a hall that had open archways leading to four other bedrooms and a closed-door marked as the bathroom.

"Did you live here before?" I asked cautiously, stepping inside, gliding my hand over the table in the middle of the living room made of smooth pine wood.

"That's what I said, or are you going deaf?" I shot him a glare before walking into the kitchen to search for some food.

The supplies were more minimal than I expected. Although it still had more items than I'd expect from an abandon house. Besides a short oval table, a long stone counter, a tall bucket, a window above the bucket and a handful of floating shelves- there wasn't much here. Well, if you don't count the cobwebs and thick coat of dust.

I'm not going to find anything in here.

Letting out a sigh, I walked back into the living room, looking around for a place that wasn't caked in dust to sit.

Absently, I heard Singer's footsteps going outside. Looking out the open back door, I could see Singer holding his palms up in front of him, his back to me, and his head tilted downward slightly. He held that position for about a minute before taking out a small vial from his pouch. Opening it, he sprinkled the contents across the ground before placing the cap back on and walking inside, closing the door behind him as the last remnants of the setting sun shined on his back. Our eyes connected for a moment before his narrowed.

"What do you want- a cookie?"

"What were you doing out there?"

"It's called magic stray. If you haven't noticed, I can do that." Rolling my eyes, I made my way to one of the bedrooms. "I hope you know that one is mine, and I will be sleeping in it."

"Then I'll stay in another one!"

"They don't have beds."

"You're so difficult!"

***

An hour after the last rays of sunlight burned out, I could see but mostly hear the ogres moving around outside. Some standing at the barrier, Singer made testing its strength to see if they could breakthrough.

Their fat round bellies swayed as they walked, a giant club or ax settled in their hands. The two nearly hidden beady eyes gleamed in the moonlight. After a moment, they decided that breaking the barrier was pointless and left.

"So, that's what an ogre looks like?" I whispered to myself. The sound of bedsheets moving had me glancing at the side as Singer sat up in his bed, letting out an annoyed, exaggerated groan.

"What are you doing making so much noise?"

"I was watching the ogres."

"Then, watch them quieter." He deadpanned, falling back down onto the bed and pulling the covers over his head. I stared at his covered form for a moment, a thought that has plagued my mind since our time together began nipping at my consciousness until I had no choice but to blurt it out.

"Have you ever seen the fairy queen?" He didn't make a move to show that he heard me. "I mean, is she- does she exist?" A groan of utter frustration left his lips as he slowly sat up, resigning himself to the conversation.

"No, I haven't," I grunted in acknowledgment, turning my attention back outside.

So, she might not be real, after all?

"But, I have met the fairy king." My eyes rolled back towards him, curiosity shining in them that I'm sure he noticed if the moan of irritation he let out was any hint.

"When?"

"If I tell you, will you go to bed and stop being so annoying?"

"I've tried to go to sleep, but my mind won't let me."

"Even though I don't care, I have to ask due to certain obligations my mother has placed on me so… why can't you sleep?" It sounded like it pained him to say the words.

"Nightmares." I simply answered, my gaze shifting away from him. He snorted, turning so his back leaned against the headboard. A sigh broke through his lips.

"I'll tell you the story, but you can't say a word." I hummed my acknowledgment, my eyes finding their way back to the window. "Well, I met him when I was nine. We were still living here then. Claribel and Eallair were just toddlers, driving my mother crazy with how much energy they had. She spent most of her time watching them. My father was away quite a bit putting up protective barriers considering there was a large ogre den around here.

"During this particular month, Favian and his parents were with us. I don't remember why, but our parents became close friends. Something about saving someone from an attack or whatever. Anyway, one day our fathers told us that they were going to find a new, safer home along the border of the forest. With our fathers gone and our mothers busy, there wasn't anyone really watching me and Favian. Keeping in mind that the two of us were young boys and taking care of little whiny brats was nowhere near our expertise, we decided to go exploring. At some point, our tiny naïve brains decided it would be a fantastic idea to go inside the ogre den to see one.

"Thankfully, we had enough common sense to know to not just rush inside. Everyone knows that ogres are vicious, vile beast that like to eat little kids for dessert. So, we snuck inside and hid. The cave had a steep drop creating a sort of cliff. The ogres stayed in the crater beneath it with nothing but a bonfire to roast their victims. Anyway, we watched them for a while, and, for one stupid reason or another, I moved and got my foot caught in a snare. Who knew ogres had enough brainpower to set up booby traps?

"Anyway, I was caught, and I couldn't get my foot free. Favian tried to help, but we weren't awesome back then like we are now. So, I made him leave to get our mothers. Favian, being who he is, didn't want to leave me alone to die, but I convinced him to go. By that time, the ogres heard us talking and came after me but, being the genius that I am, I remembered an elusive spell my father taught me to make myself blend into my environment. Performing the spell, I stayed still and watched as those hideous beasts came out. Even though they couldn't find me, they could smell me. So, having the tiny brains that they do, they just started smashing the floor, hoping to squash me at the very least.

"They came close to killing me- very close. When one was just about to bring his ax down on top of me, a blast of light energy hit him, knocking him away. That's when I heard the sound of a man speaking. He asked them what they were doing. They said they were looking for whatever was caught in their trap. I'm pretty sure he knew where I was because he looked directly at me- he even smirked! He told the ogres that he tripped the alarm because he wanted to know what would happen if he did. The ogres were going to attack him, but I guess after getting a good feel of his insanely powerful magical aura, they backed off and scurried back into their hole.

"When they were gone, he came to me, released me from the trap, and carried me home. When we were at the edge of the barrier, he left me and began walking away, but I couldn't have that. A cool fairy walking away before I could learn their name? Unacceptable. So, I called him back and asked him who he was. He told me that he's a fairy with too much time on his hands. As he was leaving, dark purple lights brightened his path before he vanished as if he walked through a portal." Pausing, he turned a smirk to me and announced dramatically, "and that's when I knew he was the fairy king. Now go to sleep." With that, he flopped back on the bed and covered himself with the blanket with a sense of finality. A laugh escaped my throat as I shook my head.

"You're such a child."

"Hey- bedtime, now!"

***

I woke with a jolt, confusion overcoming me as I looked around me. Was I asleep? Why didn't I have a nightmare, or at least feel terror from the aftermath of one? I haven't been able to sleep peacefully like this since the day Captain Jin gave me those herbs. *Bang!* I screamed in sheer fright, crashing on the floor in my terror-stricken state. When I was able to calm down enough, I scanned my surroundings cautiously, not too surprised to find I was on the second bed in Singer's room. It wasn't until my eyes connected with a beyond amused purple pair that I relaxed a little bit.

What was that bang?

The sight of a now crushed peanut shell scattered messily on Singer's nightstand, a hammer within the fairy's grasp, and a smirk on his face had my blood boiling over.

"What are you doing?" I gritted out between clenched teeth, rising to my feet.

"I was hungry and wanted a peanut."

"Why would you do that when you knew I was sleeping?"

"You're awake now, aren't you?"

"That's not the point!"

"What does it matter anyway? You were going to wake up at some point, why not now?"

Inhale… exhale.

"You know what, forget it." I sighed, turning my back to him to straighten out the mess I made of the bed.

"You're welcome, by the way."

"What are you talking about?" I asked, staying focused on my task.

"You're nightmares didn't just go away by themselves." I paused, turning around, my eyes narrowed.

"You did something?"

"No, a random good-hearted fairy came by and did it." I blinked at him, ignoring his blatant insult to my intelligence, allowing a small smile to appear on my face.

"Thank you, Singer."

"Don't get all cheesy with me. I only did it because my mother would kill me if she found out I let her precious human collapse from fatigue and get killed." I rolled my eyes, turning back around to finish my work, a stupid smile on my face.

"I need a bath. I'm starting to stink." I absently said fluffing the pillow back out before dusting my hands off, satisfied with my work.

"You always reek."

"Thank you so much for your kind words." I sarcastically spat, turning and walking out of the room.

"You should know by now I'm never going to stop being the amazing person that I am."

"Good to know." He cracked a smirk before he led the way out of the cottage.

We walked for a few minutes until we came to a small crystal-clear lake with a large oak tree with low hanging branches nearly touching the lake's surface. Singer motioned me towards the lake while he climbed a limb in the tree a few feet in the air. Eyeing the water suspiciously, a picture of a scaly woman hissing threateningly popped into my mind.

"Are there any sirens in this water like last time?" I called up to him. An annoyed groan was my response.

"Do you see any?"

"No."

"Then there isn't any! Geeze, you're so paranoid."

"How am I supposed to trust you?"

"Foolish little- fairies can't lie, you dimwitted stray!" He yelled back at me. I huffed, moving to the water and kneeling beside it.

"Excuse me for not knowing that," I mumbled to myself, getting to work. After splashing my face a few times, I felt refreshed and energized.

"So, where are we going now, stray?"

"How am I supposed to know?"

"Didn't we have this discussion yesterday? We can't find the fairy queen unless you have an epiphany, but with your level of understanding, I'm going to be stuck with you forever."

"I do know what I want- I don't know how much clearer I can be about it!" I shouted back, sending him a glare before turning my gaze back to my reflection in the lake.

Do I know what I want?

A sharp pain on the back of my head gained my attention as I rubbed the forming knot. Whirling around, fire burning in my eyes, I saw an innocent-looking acorn lying next to me.

What the-?

Another pain, this time on my forehead, had me shooting daggers at the man with a hand full of acorns preparing to chuck another one at me.

"What are you doing?" I hollered, getting to my feet.

"I'm trying to knock an epiphany into that thick rock you call a head, you foolish stray!" He yelled back, throwing another acorn, hitting me square in the forehead. I squeaked in pain, cradling my abused head, sending him a glare.

"Stop throwing things at me!"

"At least let me knock the foolishness out!"

"Stop!"

"Then, have an epiphany already!"

"You're a jerk!"

"I never denied it!" With a frustrated scream, I whirled on my heels and marched further down the lake away from him before plopping back down. The stinging of tears suddenly hit me before I found myself bawling into my hands.

Why am I crying? Didn't I tell myself I wouldn't cry anymore? I know what I want to ask the fairy queen, so why isn't she here? Why am I s*till* being denied the answers that I want? I want to know why my family was killed- why they were taken from me. So why?

"Are you still being ignorant over there?"

"Leave me alone, you heartless harpy!"

"I'm a fairy, not a harpy."

"I don't care!" The feeling of Singer's hand curling around my chin in a vice grip, forcing me to stare into his uncharacteristically cold purple eyes, shocked me into utter silence.

"But you do care because that's just who you are. You don't care that I'm mean or that I do things that can cause harm to others, you only care if it will cause harm to *you*. You're selfish, and you only truly want to know the answers to questions that concern *you*. The sooner you realize that the sooner I can go home." He released me and stood up, my eyes never leaving his. "I'll be in my tree, stay here and brood all you want." And with that, he turned around and went back to the oak.

"I'm… selfish?" *but that can't be!* How is it selfish of me to want to know why my family was killed? How is it selfish of me to risk my life to figure out what my family has that Layne felt it necessary to murder them all? How- my eyes widened as a thought sunk into my brain, burying itself there so I won't ever forget.

The night when Hawk attacked the first time, why did he go after Aric first? My room is closer to the stairs, and he surely knew I was inside, so why didn't he kill me? Why did he deliberately go after Aric? Even after, he went downstairs to go after my parents instead of me. Why would Hawk do that?

"Why did he leave me alive?" a cold chill ran down my spine. Lifting my head, I saw the lake freeze over, a horde of glowing lights floating leisurely above it leading across it into the woods.

"Would you look at that?" Singer mused, appearing behind me, his arms folded across his chest with pride. "It looks like throwing acorns at you did knock an epiphany into your head."

XV

"What happens when we get to the end of the trail?" I asked Singer, keeping a tight grip on his shirt as we followed the path of glowing sprites through the forest. For some reason, Singer was completely unperturbed by this whole creepy scenario.

"First of all, they are called pixies and should be very offended by your word choice. Second, how else do you expect to find the fairy queen?" I shot him a glare before focusing my attention on the balls of light surrounding us.

Looking closer, I can see the form of a… child?

Are these children?

Leaning towards the closest one to me, I squinted. Sure enough, I could make out the sight of a small girl- no older than seven- smiling with her eyes closed. Her face was the picture of tranquility as she just floated around almost childishly.

"What are-?"

"Hush." He barked, coming to a halt. I snorted, peering around him. Stepping from behind Singer, my jaw dropped.

Towering before us stood a giant oak tree alight with something I can only describe as magic. A low tune made by wind music played as faye that look like fairies dancing in the tree branches like small angelic dancers. Pixies surrounded the tree swaying to the music as if they were the ones creating the heavenly tune. My breath caught in my throat once I noticed the sky. Gone was the morning sunshine being replaced by a mystical array of orange, purple, and blue creating the most breathtaking sunset I've ever seen with the pixies adding an extra layer of beauty.

"It's… beautiful." I breathe, cupping my hands as a pixie came close. The calming warmth it radiated didn't surprise me nearly as much as the light giggle it let out before floating away. A smile spread across my lips as I watched it rejoin the others around the tree, almost as if it were running off to be with friends.

"Try and stay focused, stray. You know as well as I do you have a short attention span." Ignoring the rude comment, I kept my gaze high watching the pixies, fairies, and the scenery flow together radiating magic. The stupid smile on my face grew the more I witnessed. While turning, my eyes locked onto a pixie that shone slightly brighter than those around it. As my eyes focused on its face, my heart skipped a few beats as tears pricked the back of my eyes.

"… Ricky?" The pixie's light flashed as the little boy who resembled my brother let out a childish laugh *just like Ricky's!* "Ricky." I breathe, taking a few unbalanced steps towards him.

"It seems you finally won the game, little Henryk." I distantly heard a young girl call to me, but whatever was coming out of her mouth means nothing. Right now, all I can see- all I can focus on is my baby brother before me, *not dead*!

"Ricky." I breathe, falling to my knees before his tiny glowing form.

His eyes, like the others, were closed. The pure bliss covering his chubby face could've convinced me he was sleeping.

How is he here?

The face of a young girl, maybe between the age of eight and nine, with a shock of bright red hair falling in waves down her back appeared behind him. Elongated ears poked out from both sides of her head framing her peach-colored eyes. A soft smile stretched her cherry lips as her hands rose to cup around my brother's body.

"The pixies," she started slowly, her eyes never leaving my brother, "are the souls of children who have passed on from this world but contain the spirit of a faye. They are in the transition stage to becoming full-fledged faye."

"What happens when they turn into one?" the words spilled out of my mouth before I even had a chance to process them. The girl's smile widened as she dropped her hands into her lap, turning her eyes to me.

"That depends on what the soul wants and what the heart will allow." I opened my mouth to order her to explain- to tell me what will happen to my baby brother.

I can't go on knowing my brother is somewhere out here alone!

A hand on my shoulder was the only warning I received before Singer yanked me to my feet, pulling me towards the tree. My heart dropped in panic as I fought his hold with a ferocity I've only felt once before.

I can't lose him again!

"Let me go!" I growled, snatching my shoulder from his grip. Singer turned to me, but I was already searching for the little pixie that contained my little brother's soul. My chest squeezed when I couldn't find him.

He's gone…

"What would you have done?" Slowly, I turned my attention to the girl that tried to speak to me earlier. She was around the same age as the girl I talked to just seconds before. The only difference between them is that this girl has a head of vibrant brown hair and eyes the color of fresh sand on the beach. "With the pixie, I mean, what would you have done if you had a few more minutes with him?" There were so many things I wanted to say, but the words were frozen in my throat, refusing to come out. Instead, Singer stepped up, clearing his throat dramatically.

"Enough with this small talk, brat. The stray here needs to see the fairy queen so I can go home and enjoy my life." The girl didn't even spare him a glance, her eyes never leaving mine. I swallowed, the dizziness in my head increasing under the weight of the girl's stare. The slight tug on the pouch tied to my waist alerted me to the presence of the red-haired girl, her eyes entirely focused on the other standing below the oak tree.

"Stop overwhelming the poor girl, Fawn. Hasn't she gone through enough from her journey?" She turned her smile up to me, a twinkle in her eyes that sent me on edge. "My name is Cherry. It's a pleasure to finally meet you, Jayde." Before I could say anything, she slipped her hand in mine, tugging forward. "Come on! Let's go meet the queen!" She giggled childishly. The girl named Fawn stared at her for a moment before turning her back, walking towards the tree. After taking a few steps, she seemed to dissolve from sight. A pang of fear consumed me as Cherry continued to pull me.

"It's just a portal stray, calm down." Singer chided, shoving me a little. The next second, I felt a pinch as my body dissolved before reappearing in front of a pair of towering crystal doors. A carving of obsidian double bells at the tip of where they conjoined stood out prominently against the thick snow falling heavily. My skin prickled at the biting cold that surrounded us. Before I could bring it up, Cherry and Fawn both erupted into a fit of excited giggles bouncing around anxiously.

"We're here! We're here!" They shouted, taking both Singer and me by the hand, dragging us towards the doors. Shoving them aside quickly, they gasped in utter elation and adoration.

I took a moment to allow my eyes to wander the room. To put it into words wouldn't do it any form of justice. It was just… *magnificent!* Healthy, bright green vines wrapped around the walls, ceiling, and floor. Fully bloomed flowers of all types ranging from roses to daffodils sprouted along the tendrils. A set of stairs lifted a throne made of pure crystal in the middle of the back wall. On the steps lay a sleeping girl with dark green hair. There were even two trees with white trunks on either side of the throne with vines wrapping around it. What took the attention from all of this is the woman sitting on the throne.

She held beauty that put the room to shame. Her flowing dark hair framed her body as she lounged, utterly relaxed. The trademark fairy ears sticking out of her hair were pierced with red and emerald jewels from the tip to the base. Her eyes were what really mesmerized me as they held rings of different colors. The first being an outer circle of dark purple, then a circle of pink, then white, then ending with her pupil surrounded in a brilliant sky blue. Thick full lashes framed those unique eyes, a teasing smile lying on her blood-red lips.

"Welcome, young Henryk." She sweetly called, her eyes drifting towards Singer standing indifferently beside me. "Welcome to you as well, young fairy."

"Hello, yourself, boss lady." I elbowed Singer roughly in the side, shooting him a disapproving glare.

"You should be more formal when speaking to a queen, idiot!" I hissed before straightening, turning my gaze back to the amused smile of the fairy who couldn't be anyone else but the fairy queen.

Raising her hand, she motioned for us to come closer. As we did, the doors behind us closed shut. Cherry and Fawn ran to her, leaving a trail of giggles in their wake. Instead of jumping on her, they knelt beside her throne, laid their heads on the armrests, and closed their eyes.

All that excitement, just to go to sleep?

"I do not care for formality with those under my rule. I know who Singer is, so I don't expect anything less from him." Her attention then fell on Singer, "How is your family, my dear?"

"Better than I am." He scoffed, crossing his arms. "I've been spending the past week with this annoying stray, and I can't go home without her, or else my mother will torture me in a way I'd rather not think about." A light chuckle left her lips before she nodded, turning her attention to me.

"How is your family, my dear?"

"You should already know they're no longer alive."

"I only know what is whispered to me." She petted Fawn's head, gently eliciting a soft sigh from the girl. "Now, what is it that you wish of me?" taking a deep breath, I took a small step forward standing tall.

"I want to know what was so important that cost my family their lives."

"I'm afraid I can't grant you that wish."

"Why not!" I screamed, my eyes wide open.

This can't be happening!

"I can't grant you a wish that has already been fulfilled."

"What are you talking about?"

"So you've been residing here all this time? I'm impressed you've avoided detection for so long." A chill ran down my spine as I swirled around.

The sight of Layne standing before me holding a pistol towards my head was not what shook me to my core. It wasn't even the army of men behind him. What made me want to curl in a ball and hide was the hauntingly familiar sight of Hawk standing only a few feet away. Layne waved his gun to the side, a sadistic smirk playing on his lips.

"Step aside, unless you want to meet your parents." A nasty glare formed on my face, but the threatening sight of the guns his men held tighter in anticipation struck fear into my heart. Moving out of the way, I kept my glare plastered on the vile man as he walked forward, pointing his gun at the fairy queen who seemed unperturbed by his arrival.

"Welcome, traveler. What has brought you to my domain?" she asked, a welcoming smile on her face.

"I want you to grant me my wish, fairy queen."

"You may call me Bellatrix." She chirped, propping her elbow on the throne's armrest, lying her head loosely against her closed fist.

"As you wish, Bellatrix," Layne gritted out in a near hiss, "I wish for the jewel."

"I'm afraid you'll have to be more specific than that. There are many jewels in this world."

"You know what I want!" He screamed suddenly, his eyes shining with a wildfire. "I want the jewel that Jaxon Henryk wished for you to give him centuries ago- the jewel with the power to control any breathing being in this world- the jewel that is now in your possession! I want it!" That's what this is about- a stupid fairytale?

My family was killed over a fairytale!

"If you know all of that, then you should know that I can't give it to you while a Henryk lives." My heart stopped.

"That's why…" My voice hitched as a tear fell down my cheek.

"You will grant me my wish! Even if I have to spill this insect's blood on your floors- I will have it!" In his craze, he whipped the gun towards me, his finger prepared to pull the trigger, but, for some reason, he didn't. It wasn't until a thin line of blood fell from the corner of his lips that I knew something was wrong. In the next second, he fell face-first to the ground revealing Hawk standing in his place with a bloody knife in his hand.

"I would like to… apologize, your grace." He gave Bellatrix a sweeping bow. Pulling out a handkerchief from his coat, he wiped the knife clean. "For the mess, I mean." He quickly motioned to Layne's body.

"There is no need for your apologies." She smiled, straightening in her seat, her eyes glued to Hawk. "What is it that you wish?"

"It's quite simple actually, I want the jewel that my former employer has asked for." He began to pace the room, dropping the soiled handkerchief on Layne's cold body. "I admit, I was skeptical of its existence, but I knew if I left the girl alive, I would know of its authenticity. Now that I see you are real, then it must be true."

"No!" Both turned to me as well as Singer who stood tensely behind Hawk. "You can't have it! If my family died for this stupid thing- then I won't be the one to hand it over to you!" A smirk formed on his lips.

"But, it's my wish." A deafening bang filled my ears before a searing pain spread throughout my stomach.

A coldness overtook me as I felt my body fall. Darkness lined my vision as a glowing light appeared in front of Hawk. The last thing I saw before darkness took over was a blinding light and Singer standing in front of me.

XVI

A pain in my stomach woke me. Every time I breathe, it burned. A groan left my lips as a refreshing, moist cloth touched my forehead. My eyes slowly opened, revealing Lilly leaning over me with a jar of green paste in her hands. When she noticed that I was awake, a smile formed on her lips.

"I'm glad you're finally conscious." She cooed, setting the jar on the side table, grabbing a cup filled with a warm liquid.

She helped me lift my head so I could take a sip of it, soothing my dry throat. After that, I was finally able to take a painless breath. With that over, I allowed my eyes to wonder. It was then that I noticed a gardenia, still a young bud, lying on the table as healthy as it would be if it was in the ground.

"What is that?" I rasped. Lilly glanced at what I was looking at before understanding dawned on her.

"That was in your pocket when Singer brought you here."

"I didn't-"

"That's what happens to pixies when they are in their dormant state," Singer called from the doorway. It was this point that I realized that I was in a room. Maybe in their house? "I'm pretty sure that Cherry brat put it there."

Was it when she tugged my pocket?

Sensing my confusion, Lilly gave me a pitying smile.

"Until the spirit turns into a faye or moves on, it will remain a pixie or in its budding flower." I swallowed glancing at the bud. So... for now my brother will be with me?

"What happened…?"

"Well," Singer started seemingly knowing what I was talking about. "Since you died, for like, a minute, every Henryk was technically dead, so Hawk was able to get the jewel. So now the psychopath is back in Clearapal using it to recruit people to his army."

"Army?"

"There are whispers." Lilly started. "That the humans are declaring war on all faye." My heart stopped beating, and my breath hitched.

No… no!

"I have to stop it." I tried to sit up, but the burning increased tenfold, forcing me back down to the bed.

"Rest." Lilly scolded, placing a hand on my shoulder.

"Besides, what do you expect to do to him? Nag him until he shoots you again?" I glared at Singer.

"I'll think of something, but I can't- I won't sit around and do nothing!" There was silence in the room before a smile spread across Lilly's face.

"Well, it seems you two will be having more bonding time together!" She clasped her hands together, a happy smile on her face. The pain-filled groan of despair that followed was in stark contrast to her happy squeal.

"I'm going to be stuck with that annoying stray forever."

ABOUT THE AUTHOR

Jordan Walker is an aspiring author in North Carolina. Walker grew up as a military child. Her father is a retired Navy veteran, and her mother is a DECA employee. Walker also has two older siblings who are both serving in the U.S Air Force and a younger brother in elementary school. Walker has a BBA in Management and currently works as a Business Analyst. *Dark Nights* is Walker's second published work.

www.ingramcontent.com/pod-product-compliance
Ingram Content Group UK Ltd.
Pitfield, Milton Keynes, MK11 3LW, UK
UKHW041829200726
13854UKWH00002BA/894